RISE OF THE KING

A Bird Shifter Novel

MANDY M. ROTH

King of Prey Series

King of Prey
A View to a Kill
Master of the Hunt
Rise of the King
Prince of Pleasure
Prince of Flight

Blurb

Rise of the King (King of Prey)
Book four in the King of Prey series.

Warrior, bastard, outcast, traitor to his
kind, these are all labels Lazar has worn
for the past several years, since he took a
stand against the actions of a mad king.
He's defended the Kingdom of the Hawks
even though the blood of the Falcons runs
through his veins. He's bedded their
women, drank their mead and protected
their king. None of that makes him one of
them. An empty pit has been in his
stomach for years, believing his true mate
perished long ago. When he learns she's

alive, he has to not only win her over, but also make her understand men who can shift into birds aren't the things of nightmares. They're real, and he's one of them.

Sabrina lives a relatively sheltered life. Her overprotective uncle means well but can sometimes go too far. When he shows up with a sexy hunk she's dreamed about, it's all Sabrina can do to control her emotions. As old lies are uncovered, she has to decide if she should open her heart to a man who has made using women an art form and who also happens to have wings. Plus, he's more than just any old shifter male. He's the rightful king of the Falco, and it's time he rose to his position and accepted his destiny, even if that destiny includes her.

Prologue

Accipitridae Realm

Lazar drew the beauty below him closer. He knew the minute he woke she would be gone. Her deep brown eyes stared up at him. Her full rosy lips beckoned to him. He kissed them again, having long since memorized the feel of them. He didn't want to ever wake. Here, in his dreams, he had her.

Sabrina.

His mate.

In waking hours he had only emptiness in his chest. In reality his mate had perished long ago, never able to grow into the beauty below him. Her life had been cut short.

He held tighter to her, his tongue moving around hers. Their naked forms slid against one another, and his cock hardened once more. It wanted in her as much as he wanted to be in her. She was paradise. His salvation. She was what the women in his reality weren't.

Perfect.

She made the slightest sound of pleasure as he lined up with her wet core. "Open for me," he said.

She did.

Lazar snapped awake, alone in his bedchamber. He stared up at the red material draped around the four-post wooden bed. With a huge, exasperated breath, he closed his eyes, his cock hard with lust. He tossed aside the remaining covers and lay there, totally exposed and totally nude.

He thumped his head on his pillow. He wanted to fall back asleep. He wanted to return to his dreams of her—of his mate. At least the mate his mind dreamed up for him.

His cock was too full of need to allow him to drift off again. With a sigh, Lazar sat up and grabbed a dark green loincloth. He wrapped it and secured it with a broach indicating his rank among the guards, as was customary to his kind. He eyed his chamber door and stood. With a heavy heart he moved toward it, knowing he'd search out a serving wench in the castle to satisfy his needs. He hated that weakness. What he hated more was dreaming of a woman he could never have.

Chapter One

The sun, near setting, edged over the crenels of the castle walls. Each gap let the sun's rays shine through directly into Lazar's eyes. He took a moment to adjust to the change in light levels. The pattern the rays cast onto the training yards was captivating.

Lazar pushed his hair from his face and spun, bringing his sword up to block his opponent's strike. The shock reverberated through his arms. His muscular, trained body absorbed it with relative ease. The blow was hard and no practice weapons were used, so steel-on-steel sounds echoed throughout the training yard.

Since they were but fledglings, the bird shifters' males practiced with real weapons. No sense learning if what you were learning with could no more hurt an insect, let alone protect you. As they'd grown into fierce adult males, they'd only perfected the art of battle and swordplay. They conditioned many hours, never allowing their skills to waver. One never knew when one would require them.

The man coming at him had oddly become something of a friend over the course of Lazar's last several years within the Kingdom of the Hawks. Sachin, once someone Lazar would have seized the moment to kill rather than train alongside, turned lightly on his feet, moving with the grace of a true warrior. Lazar drew upon his abilities as a seasoned fighter and twisted, going at his opponent. He nicked Sachin's arm. Something that didn't happen often.

Sachin raised a brow, and a mischievous grin slipped over his face. His amused silver gaze locked on Lazar. "Good one."

"Are you bleeding?" a shrill, feminine voice demanded from the sidelines, interrupting the sparring.

Wisely, both men lowered their weapons as Sachin's mate, Paige, approached the training yard. She eyed her husband and pointed to his upper arm. The tiniest trickle of blood was evident.

It was only a scratch, but from her expression it was life-threatening. "You're hurt."

Sachin scoffed. No man worth his salt would cry foul over a nick such as the one Lazar had given him. It was easy to see the warrior was insulted anyone would attempt to do so on his behalf. That being said, the person doing it was his wife, his mate and a fine balance had to be maintained. "'Tis a scratch, my love."

Paige put a hand on her hip and glared at him, her brown eyes going hard. Her auburn hair spilled over her creamy, pale shoulders. She looked both lovely and slightly like a witch about to cast a thousand poxes upon them all. Lazar guessed the latter, for her temper knew no bounds.

"A scratch, my ass," she sputtered. "You were supposed to be back home for dinner nearly two hours ago, and here I find you horsing around with your buddy and bleeding all over the place?"

It took a moment for Lazar to wrap his mind around all Paige had said. Her human slang often left most of the men of the realm blinking in confusion until they surmised her meaning. Sachin cast Lazar an apologetic look. "It would appear our training has ended for the day."

"You're damn right it's ended," his wife snapped. She was feisty to say the least.

Lazar failed to hide his laughter as the head of the guards took a verbal lashing from a woman nearly half his size. Paige rounded on Lazar. "Think this is funny? Wait until you're mated and we women gang up on you. You won't be snickering then, bucko."

Sachin laughed deeply. "That would be a sight."

Huffing, Lazar puffed out his chest. He had no desire to be stuck with one woman and one woman only. "No offense, but I'd much rather sample many women than tie myself to one."

"Watch what you say in front of my wife," Sachin said sternly. "You will not speak of women with ill reputations before her."

Rolling her eyes, Paige snorted and waved her hand in the air. "Oh please. We all know Lazar's reputation with the ladies —if you can call them that. And I'm hardly a blushing virgin anymore."

Lazar wagged his brows, feeling victorious and oddly proud of his reputation.

Sachin jutted out his chin. "I was as you are once, friend. Mark my words. When you meet your mate, everything changes."

Tightness gripped Lazar's chest. His mate had perished over twenty years ago, taking with her his chance at happiness. He plastered a smile to his face, pushing down old feelings of sorrow and regret. They had no place in his life anymore, and there was naught he could do to change the past. It was etched in stone, and he was sentenced to a life without love.

Already his nights were spent dreaming of a woman who did not exist. His days could not be filled with such foolishness as well. The subject wasn't one he'd broach with Sachin or anyone from the Kingdom of the Hawks. It was personal, and it was no use bringing up that which could not be changed. "I am sure you are correct."

Paige shooed Sachin off and followed behind him, continuing to scold him the entire way. Other guards looked away, knowing they'd catch hell from the head of the guards at a later date if they dared acknowledge their commander's humiliation at the hands of his tiny wife.

Lazar debated returning to the castle to search for one of the kitchen maids again. After waking from his erotic dream, he'd sought one out and fucked her. And he'd taken two in the buttery only yesterday.

Slow week.

He rubbed his upper chest, his hands

skimming over the scratch marks the one he'd fucked today had left. They served as a reminder that while the women of the kingdom sought his cock and toned body, they hated what he was—a falcon shifter. The scratches hadn't been made in the height of passion as a sign of a good time had by all, but rather made to spite him, to spit in his face as to what he was—a falcon shifter. Not a hawk shifter—his nemeses for the majority of his life. Sadly, the scratches paled in comparison to the scars he bore. They were recaps of times best not thought upon.

The kitchen maid from earlier had been wild and wanted him for his body and his skilled cock but didn't want the stigma attached to him—enemy, falcon, outsider. The scratches she'd inflicted were all but healed over. The long soak he'd taken in the hot springs had helped, along with washing away her scent. He found it unpleasant, as he did a lot of the females from the region. They weren't *his* kind.

Glancing around the empty training yard, Lazar drew in a deep breath and let his wings emerge. There was the smallest of pinches in his lower back before his huge wings spanned out and around him. He flexed them, enjoying the feeling of being free. Too long he'd gone between flights. He launched into the air—the need to fly out his aggressions was great. The wind whipped past him, lifting his hair and cooling his aching muscles. He closed his eyes a moment, savoring the feeling.

When he finally landed, it was with a grand view of the kingdom. He sat on his haunches, peering out and over the valley below. It was beautiful, as was most of the realm. The buildings were constructed in a way that didn't totally take from the land-scape—unlike the human realm where skyscrapers and pavement appeared to be all one could see for miles and miles. Humans cared little about preserving the beauty around them. They seemed to want things taller, faster, quicker. Nothing was good enough for them, and one day their hunger for more would be their downfall.

The Kingdom of the Hawks was grand, spanning over most of the

Northern Region of Accipitridae. Some of the homes within it had been built around trees. It wasn't unheard of to enter a villager's home to find a large trunk within and ample light streaming in from many an opening. His kind, the bird shifters, didn't like to feel captured or caged within their dwellings. They liked the feel of the sun on their faces and the smell of fresh air.

Not so long ago, he'd thought of the kingdom's occupants as the sworn enemy —the *Buteo Regalis*—the most hated of all the enemies of his kind.

The *Falco Peregrinus*.

He'd once been a proud member of his kind and a fierce warrior for the cause. It was a cause he'd been led to believe was just and true. He should have known better. Everything that had sprung forth from the mouth of the king of the Falco had been a lie, so why shouldn't the truth about the *Buteo Regalis* be as well?

He'd been following the ramblings of a man hell-bent on power and ruling all the realm. Had he stood his ground and fought for his birthright, the Falco wouldn't be feared by all and thought of as the enemy to nearly all the varying kingdoms within the bird-shifter realm. No, Lazar would not have ruled with fear and lies. He would have ruled very, very differently.

Events and circumstances had left Lazar branded a traitor among his people. He clenched his fists, silently swearing to exact revenge on those who had claimed what was rightfully his.

Here, among the *Buteo Regalis*, or more commonly known to humans as royal hawks, he was trusted by the king yet feared and looked down upon by many of the king's subjects. If they knew the truth of who he was, his actual birthright, they'd not only fear him, they'd see him on the end of a pike, rotting, for all to know what they did to those who crossed them.

Until that time came, he would continue to fight for their cause, fuck their women and drink his fair share of their mead. He'd never been able to pass up a good time. That trait was seen as a flaw by many, himself included.

Movement from the village below caught his eye. He tilted his head to watch as a warrior he'd seen at the castle often enough wandered into the darkened woods surrounding the village. He headed in the direction of a portal to the human realm. Curiosity got the better of Lazar, and he remained perched in place, wondering what would make a man act in such a manner, especially considering that King Kabril had yet to lift the bans on traveling between the realms, and Gardelle was certainly a strict follower of Kabril's rules.

Gardelle was one of the few guards at the castle who spoke to Lazar without a touch of malice in his voice. Never did the man mention trips to the human realm, though. Lazar's love of visiting the human realm was well-known. So was his desire to break rules. So far, Kabril had only made a few comments regarding the manner, mostly to warn him against being seen in flying form by humans. It wasn't like the king had much in the way of credibility when it came to the old rule of no contact with humans, since his new wife and now queen to the hawks was in fact human. So was Sachin's wife, Kabril's head advisor. Lazar chuckled as he thought about Paige's hold over the feared head of the guards.

Lazar caught sight of Gardelle through a tiny clearing in the canopy of the trees. When Gardelle shifted forms, allowing his wings to emerge, Lazar did the same. He backed into a recessed area as the warrior flew by heading straight for the portal to the human realm.

Waiting until the right moment, Lazar remained in place until the object of his curiosity passed before emerging from his hiding spot. He took to flight, soaring above the Tocallie Mountain peaks. Gardelle passed through one of the many portals nestled in the serene area, and so did Lazar, careful to keep a reasonable distance to avoid drawing suspicion.

Gardelle traveled far, and since the human realm had already fallen into darkness for the night, it was difficult to see exactly where the man was going without following closer. Lazar increased his speed, knowing that as a Falco Warrior, he possessed speed greater than that of any Hawk Warrior. He regained a visual on the warrior, following close, assuming Gardelle would do as many other warriors did when visiting the human realm—stop at the known whorehouses or seedy bars, as Lazar had once heard them called by a human.

All he knew was each time he needed his dick scratched, he simply flew to one of them. The women there always seemed more than willing to serve his needs, and none held what he was against him because they didn't know. To them he was simply a man, not a shifter. Something that was far from the truth.

Chapter Two

SABRINA TOSSED AWAY THE COVERS AND eased out of bed. Her body was in a heightened state of arousal. Dreams, filled once again with pleasures provided by a mysterious lover, consumed her sleep.

Her chest grew tight as she thought of her dream lover. One she could never remember the face of, yet she knew every inch of his body. His voice was engraved into her soul. She slipped on her silk robe in a trancelike state, her mind still focused on her dream lover.

The French doors leading to the balcony were open, and a brisk breeze filtered through them. She shivered as she headed toward the doors. The thin white nightgown she wore did little to protect her from the cool air. Her nipples hardened, and gooseflesh appeared on her arms. Nothing would deter her from her goal, feeling the full night air upon her face.

She crept onto the balcony and soaked in the beauty of the night. While it wasn't that late, the days had grown shorter because of the time of the year. The moon was partially hidden, making the light low, but it was enough to allow her to see at least somewhat. She approached the railing and pressed her palms to it, closing her eyes and tipping her head back. The wind lifted her long, dark hair, whipping it around her pale face. The smallest of smiles touched her lips, and the urge to experience even more freedom came over her.

Many a night she'd had dreams similar to this—where she sought out the urge to feel the wind upon her face and fought the urge to attempt flight. As she'd done hundreds of times before, *in her dreams*, Sabrina lifted her nightgown and proceeded to climb onto the lowest rung of the railing, unafraid of being three stories high. If anything, she was disappointed she wasn't higher. She stood, managing to steady herself easy enough, her eyes still closed tight. She put her arms out wide, simulating flying, and tipped her head back.

The breeze moved past her, over her face, and she smiled, thinking back to her dreams of her mysterious lover. One with wings. In her dreams they'd fly to various locations, exotic ones, in a place that wasn't like Earth. It was better. Far better.

The wind picked up, becoming harsher than expected. She faltered a bit, still staying upright. Her robe blew up and out, acting as a cape or even wings. Though she couldn't actually fly, in her mind she was soaring. The wind caught hold of her robe, yanking it free of her. It took flight, and she opened her eyes in time to try to reach for it.

A mistake.

———

LAZAR EASED BACK from his pursuit of the male warrior as Gardelle descended at a rapid rate. The man landed on a rooftop of a very large human dwelling, his wings receding into his back quickly, leaving no sign of having been there. With a shake of his head, Gardelle sent long waves of dark hair tumbling over his shoulders. The warrior glanced back, and Lazar spotted the long scar running from just under the man's right eye to the man's chin. It was the after mark of a talon. Lazar had several on his back and chest and knew what the scars they left behind looked like. He'd seen others on the faces of men. The scarring resulted from going too long without proper healing, or if tainted soil made its way into the wound and it wasn't cleaned properly or fast enough.

Gardelle opened a set of red doors and entered the home, obviously having been there before. The dwelling was certainly bigger than many Lazar had seen humans live within. Curious, Lazar found an old, oversized tree and perched, observing silently. A flash of movement caught his attention, something white fluttering in the breeze. Tipping his head, he spotted a woman tumbling from a balcony on another level. Something deep within, something primitive, took the lead, forcing him from his spot. He dove, his speed impressive to say the least. Without thought, he put his arms out and grabbed hold of the young woman, harder than he'd have liked.

"Harrumph," she gasped. Her long, nearly black hair blew up and around them, acting like a veil. As it fell backward and revealed her face to him, his entire body tensed. It was her.

The woman he'd dreamed of.

Her chocolate-brown eyes widened with fright as she made a strange noise. Did she squeak like a mouse?

"I have you," he said softly.

He tightened his hold on her as blood rushed through his veins and straight to his cock. He inhaled her sweet scent. It had been imprinted upon him in his dreams. He'd often wake and instantly miss it.

His mind raced with all the impossibilities. He'd always assumed he'd invented the woman he'd started dreaming of some five years prior. He'd convinced himself she was his mind's way of coping with the loss of his mate—Sabrina. This woman he held was what he'd believed his mate would have grown to had she lived.

Nothing made sense. The woman he'd dreamt of was real and human? He inhaled again, trying to find a discrepancy in her scent, trying hard to sense traces of shifter on her. Was she one of them? Was she a bird shifter? He found no sign of it being true, nor did he find any scent markers to indicate she had been claimed by another shifter. Her scent stirred things in him that had not been touched before during waking hours. Yes, he sought out women to fuck and suck him, but this wasn't the same need. It was so much more. The primal need to whisk her away to a place all his own was hard to beat. His cock throbbed, and his arms naturally flexed, increasing his grip on the beauty. In his dreams he and the women shared no names, only pleasures. Endless pleasures.

She whimpered softly. The noise cut through his haze and slammed into him, pulling the very air from his lungs. He adjusted his hold on her, careful to cause her no further pain. Still the urge to flee with the female was great. Somehow, he managed to land on the same balcony she'd fallen from. Rather than bolt with her, he kept hold of her, memorizing her delicate features. Her pale pink lips puckered into an O as she continued to stare at him with shock and wonder upon her beautiful face. His skill with the ladies had never been in question, yet for the life of him he could think of nothing suave to say or do. All he could do was simply soak in the very sight of her.

"You really do have…" She paused, her voice like silk easing over his skin. "…wings."

His lips twitched with the urge to smile. "Yes, I do."

Her tiny hand went instantly to his left wing. "I know you."

"You do?" It felt as if he'd been punched in the gut. Had he not had hold of her he might very well have doubled over. Legends of old spoke of true mates being able to connect on a dream plane, but that would mean she was actually his mate, and that could not be. Sabrina was dead. She'd died as a child.

"Your voice," she responded. "I know your voice."

She stroked his wing, sending shock waves of pleasure through his system. For bird shifters, having one's wings caressed in a loving manner or by a female who already stirred one's loins was the equivalent of her hand being upon one's sex, stroking one's cock. Lazar nearly ejaculated where he stood. He would have had she not picked that moment to faint. Luckily, he still had hold of her or she would have fallen yet again.

The woman, while beautiful, had no sense.

Dipping his head, Lazar found himself inhaling her scent once more. This time his lips grazed the tender, pale skin of her neck. He knew he shouldn't steal a kiss, but he couldn't stop himself. He pressed his lips to hers and kept the kiss chaste but kissed her all the same.

She stirred slightly, and her tongue darted into his mouth. He swayed, thinking he might be the one to do the fainting as fire shot through him. He tensed before dragging her against his chest. She was like a rag doll in his arms, so limp, so pliable, yet so incredibly gorgeous. His tongue eased around hers. The kiss was familiar, just as the kisses in his dreams. He wanted to go further, take what was happening between them to the next level. Dammit if he didn't want to lower her to the ground and sink into her.

Take her. Run with her. Claim her as your own.

His inner voice was nearly overpowering, and he almost obeyed.

Her tongue continued to move with his in a steady rhythm as if they were part of the same choreographed dance. Her tiny hand moved to his cheek, and Lazar pulled her even tighter against his body. He'd crush her if he wasn't mindful of his strength and desire.

The thought sobered him. He stopped the kiss and stared down at her. Semi-lucid, she puckered her lips sweetly. So tempting. So close.

No more. You could harm her.

His sensitive hearing picked up the indication someone was coming. He glanced through the open doors and into what he guessed was her bedroom. Light shone from the hallway, and a shadow appeared, growing bigger as the sound of the footsteps deepened. Knowing better than to allow himself to be seen by yet another human, Lazar entered the woman's room and laid her gently upon the bed. She moved a touch, indicating she was close to coming to. He backed into the shadows of the room to observe. He entered a closet and kept the door propped slightly. He could not leave her presence just yet.

Mayhap not ever, he thought.

SABRINA STIRRED AWAKE, surprised to find herself in bed. With a sigh, she bent her head and thought more about it. "I dreamed I was awake? Weird."

Excitement raced through her. It felt as if she'd run a marathon. For the first time, she could remember *his* face. Her dream lover. And what a face it was. She frowned. Why was it she continued to dream of him with wings?

A knock sounded at her bedroom door before it opened partially. A pair of dark brown eyes was revealed, holding concern as was normally the case.

"Brina?" her uncle said in the best soft tone the man was capable of mustering. "It is only seven o'clock. You're in bed already?"

She sat up slowly and stared at him. "Gardelle?"

He opened the door all the way and stepped into her room. As usual, he was dressed in a suit that was partially undone, often looking like a disheveled well-to-do businessman. His long hair was pulled back at the nape of his neck. A scar marred his face, but she was used to it. It had been there her whole life, and he was still incredibly handsome even with it. He didn't talk about how he'd gotten it, and she never pried.

Happy to see him, Sabrina slipped from her bed and went to him, hugging him. He towered over her and chuckled, embracing her as well. He kissed the top of her head. "Ah, small one, I have missed you."

"Your business trip lasted longer than last time," she stated matter-of-factly. He was all the family she had, and she missed him whenever he had to be away—which seemed to be quite often as of late. The house was big and felt empty with just her in it. Wishing he could be home more didn't work, and asking yielded similar results.

He sighed, his hand coming to rest on her shoulder. "I know. I am sorry. I came as soon as I could." He stared past her at the other side of the room. "Brina, the night air is cold. Why would you leave your doors wide open? Anyone could fly in."

She blinked, sure she'd heard him wrong. "Anyone could what?"

Gardelle loosened his tie, appearing uncomfortable. "I meant, *anything* could fly into your room. Insects, *birds*, bats, anything."

She glanced in the direction of the open doors and bit at her lower lip. "I had a dream about flying again." She already knew his reaction would not be a good one.

As expected, he huffed and stormed the doors, slamming them shut with such force she wasn't sure how they didn't break. He spun around and faced her. She jerked back and bumped into her dresser. A yelp tore free of her. While she knew her uncle would never harm her, denying how imposing he looked at the moment was impossible.

Gardelle averted his gaze, composing himself. "Brina, I'm sorry. I just worry. That is all."

"Why would me having dreams about flying make you worry?" It was a legitimate question—one she'd asked many times before.

He didn't respond.

Not that she expected him to. For as well as she knew him, he was still a mystery. So much of his life he kept private from her, hiding behind the guise of work. She knew better though. There was certainly something more than met the eye when it came to Gardelle, something off, but questioning it got her nowhere. Whenever she pushed too hard, he'd leave on extended business trips as if he planned them in order to avoid answering her questions. Questions like, for starters, why he hadn't seemed to age a day in all the time he'd been her guardian. And he'd been as much since she was only three.

"Was this dream as the others were?" he questioned.

"Yes and no. This one was a little different."

"How so?" He pulled off his tie completely and stuffed it in his front jacket pocket. As nice as he always looked, he seemed uncomfortable in layers upon layers of clothing. It was as if he were dying to get out of it. Thankfully, he controlled himself.

Reaching for her robe, she smiled and then stopped. Her robe was always at the foot of her bed. Now it wasn't. She glanced around. "Odd."

"Brina?"

"My robe," she said, pointing to the end of the bed at the patterned, embroidered bedspread where her robe could normally be found. "It was there when I fell asleep. I think it grew legs and walked away."

Gardelle's gaze went from the foot of her bed to the balcony doors. "Tell me of your dream, Brina."

With a shrug, she continued. "I dreamed that I woke up from an interesting dream," she said, not wanting to tell him of her sex dreams, "and that I went out to the balcony to feel the breeze on my face."

The color drained from Gardelle's face. He swayed slightly, looking sick to his stomach. "And?"

"And." She twiddled her fingers, nerves getting the better of her. "I went onto the balcony. I had my arms out, letting the night breeze sweep over me, when I lost my footing."

"Lost your footing?" He tugged at the cuffs of his sleeves.

She squirmed in place. "Erm, did I forget to mention that in my dream I climbed onto the railing? Just the lower rung, but then the wind picked up and it caught my robe, and it just sort of lifted me when I reached for the robe. Then I fell."

His eyes widened. "What?"

Repeating it seemed unnecessary and foolish. He was already upset enough. "I didn't hit the ground," she reminded, as if it would help matters any.

Gardelle fumed as he took a step in her direction. "Have you a death wish? I have spent over twenty years protecting you only for you to leap to your death now that you're nearly twenty-four?"

"Spent what doing what?" she probed, confused. "And I wasn't leaping to my death. I was dreaming. Big difference."

"In this *dream…*" He composed himself again. "Tell me how it is you managed not to hit the ground."

"A hot guy with wings caught me." She flashed a wide smile thinking of her savior. The unique coloring of his eyes still made her chest tight. "Like the times I've had the dreams in the past and you were there, catching me before I hit the ground. But his wings were different from yours. A little anyways. My dreams really like adding those to guys. Freaky, huh?"

Gardelle pivoted, assuring the French doors were locked. He gazed intensely out the windows before pulling the curtains. When he faced her, there was no mistaking the fear in his eyes. "Tell me more of this man. What did he look like? Do you know him? Tell me it was not Latravis."

She tensed at the mention of Latravis's name. Her uncle held no love for the man, but to assume she'd dreamed of him was a bit much. Though he did fit the hot-guy description for sure. She scrunched up her face. "Why in the world would I dream about him with wings?"

Gardelle pinched the bridge of his nose, an annoyed breath leaving his body. "Latravis is not a man to toy with, Brina. Do you remember what I told you to do if he found you again?"

"Avoid open spaces, yell for help and try to be somewhere crowded," she said, ticking off his rules on her fingers as she went. It wasn't as if she actually did anything her uncle suggested in regards to Latravis. He was harmless. "I don't understand why. You don't think he'd hurt me, do you? I don't think he'd ever——"

"He'd do far more than hurt you." Gardelle approached slowly. His body language said he still struggled with his temper. "He'd take you far from here, Brina. You'd be his captive. A pawn in a game as old as time."

She couldn't help but giggle. It was small but there. "Right."

Going to her closet, she stopped, the weight of someone's stare upon her. She glanced to the side, half expecting someone to actually be there. Nothing but darkness greeted her.

Gardelle raised a hand politely. "Brina, I've told you time and time again that you're special. So is Latravis. Do not make his mission easier. He and his kind are cruel. He is a madman just as his father was before him. Power and riches long ago went to his head, taking with them his sanity."

She grabbed a new robe from the closet and slipped it on before going to Gardelle. Putting a hand on his forearm, she offered a warm smile. "Have you ever listened to yourself? At times, you talk like you just stepped out of the pages of a history book. All prim and proper."

"Brina, please. This is important." He bent slightly but was still too tall to see eye to eye with her. "Look me in the eyes and swear to me that if Latravis finds you, you'll obey my wishes."

Going to her tiptoes, she pressed a chaste kiss to his cheek. He needed to hear the words even if they were a lie. She knew as much. "I promise."

He exhaled and nodded, patting her hand. If she didn't know better, she'd have sworn he was tearing up. "Thank you." He kissed her forehead and headed for the door. "I'm going to have a look around outside."

"Why? Think there is a guy with wings lurking?" she asked, attempting to be funny. It fell flat.

"One never knows." Gardelle exited the room, shutting the door behind him.

Chapter Three

LAZAR REMAINED IN THE SHADOWS. HE
watched as Gardelle left. The warrior had
been attentive to the woman, doting on
her in a manner an older brother or even a
father might. Had Gardelle treated her in
any other manner, especially one of a
lover, Lazar wasn't sure he'd have been
able to maintain his hiding spot. His palms
already itched to touch the female again,
his body tense with longing. The idea of
another male touching her in the same
manner he desired left Lazar beside
himself with pent-up rage.

He wasn't a man to be pushed, and
anything to do with the woman would
certainly be considered pushing.

Talk of Latravis had aided in keeping Lazar in his place. When his half-brother's name had first come up, he'd nearly gasped. Gardelle had never once mentioned knowing Latravis before, at least not to Lazar. Then again, Lazar didn't exactly advertise he was the illegitimate son of the past king and rightful heir to the throne of his people either. Latravis, nearly twenty cycles less than Lazar's two hundred plus cycles, currently sat upon the throne, leading the Falcons. He was cruel and abused his power, but then again, the power was his to abuse.

It was not Lazar's as had once been promised.

A strange beeping noise came from the tiny black box on the woman's side table. She approached it and opened it. Lazar had been to the human realm enough to recognize a computer but was surprised to see how tiny they were becoming.

Humans and their belief that smaller is better.

He shook his head, adjusting his cock through his loincloth. Bigger was better, and to date, not one wench had claimed otherwise.

An image of another young woman appeared on the screen. She smiled. "Sabrina."

Lazar froze at the name.

Gardelle had called the beautiful woman Brina.

Brina. *Sabrina.*

His chest tightened. It couldn't be. The Sabrina he'd once known had died when she was but three cycles, and that was over twenty cycles ago. He stared harder at her, noting again how dark her eyes were. They were so brown that they bordered on black, just like her hair.

Just like the Sabrina he remembered.

You've dreamed of your mate. It is truly her.

He shook his head.

Impossible. She's human.

His pulse sped, and he vaguely heard the conversation taking place between Sabrina and her friend over what he'd learned not long ago was called the Internet.

The need for fresh air was great, and with Sabrina's current distraction, he made a move for the exterior doors. He acted with a speed humans did not possess and assumed himself free and clear of notice as he stepped out and onto the balcony.

Something seized hold of him, lifting him into the air. The attack came so fast that Lazar didn't even have time to allow his wings to emerge.

"Why are you here?" Gardelle demanded, spittle flying from his mouth as he yanked harder on Lazar. "Are you a spy for the Falco? Did you befriend us only to gain access to Brina? Go back and tell your king he cannot have her!"

Lazar caught hold of the warrior's wrists and held tight. "G-Gardelle, cease this. I am no spy, and Latravis is no king of mine."

Gardelle settled somewhat. "Then why are you here? And what..." he stressed, "...do you think you're doing in Brina's room?"

"I was curious when I saw you leave

the realm. I followed you and..." he tugged at Gardelle's wrists more, getting the man to ease his grip somewhat, "...Brina fell. I caught her."

He gasped. "It was real? She fell again?"

"Again?"

Calming, Gardelle flew them to the rooftop and landed, releasing Lazar in the process. "She is prone to sleepwalking."

"She seemed awake enough to me," Lazar countered. "Though she mentioned my wings and then fainted."

Gardelle came at him fast, and Lazar expected the warrior to go to blows. Instead, the man hugged him in a strange manner, almost as one would a long-lost friend or relative, and released him. "Thank you for keeping her safe."

"Who is she?"

A pregnant pause followed before Gardelle spoke. "She is my niece."

Lazar snorted. "Right. She smells of humanity. She is no shifter. Not to mention the Kingdom of Hawks has been without births until the recent ones of the two nobles and Sachin."

The look Gardelle gave Lazar made his laughter die on his tongue. "My sister was a half-sister—the product of my father's affair with a human woman. My mother was less than pleased when it came to light, and she had my sister taken from the human realm and given to your people —to the Falco—as punishment. To teach my father a lesson for daring to lie with another."

Lazar sucked in a big breath. "No."

A steely expression stole over Gardelle's face. "Yes. Much to my mother's dismay, the Falco warrior who found my sister did not run her through with his sword. He took her home to his wife who, like so many at the time, found herself barren and longing for a child to tend to."

"You're saying your sister was raised by a Falco couple?"

"Aye." He nodded. "I was already many cycles when she was born. When I learned of her existence and the circum-stances surrounding it, I went to the people who had her with the intention of taking her to raise her myself. What I found shocked me." He met Lazar's gaze and swallowed hard. "She was not only being raised by a Falco couple, she was loved and cherished by them. In addition, the couple who had taken her in were not lowborn. No. They were noble."

Lazar listened carefully.

"Brenya, my sister, grew into a beautiful woman."

The night seemed to spin around Lazar. "Brenya? As in the Brenya who passed while giving birth to a daughter some twenty-plus cycles ago? Sabrina?"

Gardelle drew back. "How is it you know this information? It is not common knowledge. Only the highest among the Falco are aware a child had been conceived. Great shame was placed upon my sister because of the man she chose to lay with. He was far from a nobleman, but they tell me he was a good man. An honest Falco man."

"But he was not Latravis," Lazar said, his words clipped. "And Latravis had decided to take Brenya to his bed. When he learned a child already quickened in her belly, he was livid. He called for her execution and that of the man she had given herself to." He remembered the day well. The young tailor whom Brenya had fallen in love with had been executed in the courtyard for all to see. Lazar had been ordered to find and kill Brenya but had disobeyed, choosing instead to take her to a safe location before fabricating her death as well.

"A warrior among the Falco took pity upon my sister and helped her escape Latravis's reach." Gardelle appeared far away in thought for a moment. "She survived him only to die in childbirth."

"No," Lazar added, a long pause hanging in the air. "She did not pass during the birth of her child. She passed directly after. She lived long enough to name the child."

"And you know this how?" Gardelle demanded, stalking towards him. He stopped in mid-motion. "*You* were there, weren't you?"

A tiny incline of the head was all that was needed.

"You look like him," Gardelle said, glancing him over. "The same eyes."

Lazar stiffened, already knowing of whom Gardelle referred to.

Latravis.

"Have no fear. Your secret is safe with me so long as you promise to keep Sabrina's existence to yourself. If Latravis finds her, he'll use her as leverage."

"Over?"

Lifting a brow, Gardelle brought attention to his scar. "You tell me, Lazar. Who would be hurt the most if Sabrina were to be taken by Latravis? If he were to impose a forced mating upon her, who would he have power over?"

"Sabrina's true mate," he answered without thought.

Gardelle stared harder at him. "And who do you think this mate might be? Think hard, Lazar. Who risked all, most likely unsure why, to assure she was born and kept from harm?"

He did.

Lazar swayed and would have fallen had Gardelle not reached out to steady him. He knew she was his mate, yet hearing it spelled out and knowing the threat that existed to her was overwhelming.

With a shake of his head, Gardelle exhaled slowly. "All this time, you have been right under my nose and I knew not you were the one I seek. A piece of me feared the rumored eldest brother would be even crueler than Latravis—that I would be handing my niece to a monster. One she was born for. You know the Oracles and their prophecies. None have been wrong yet."

Lazar's knees felt weak, and he sank to his backside on the roof, the knowledge his mate was not only alive but within the house below him too much to bear. For so long he'd thought his chance at true happiness had been ripped away, that his brother had murdered it along with so many others. Emotions bombarded him, taking root in his very soul. Everything was different now.

"I assumed Latravis had Sabrina executed while I was off on a mission," he confessed. The emotions he'd felt that day were as real now as they had been nearly twenty cycles ago. "I returned to the castle to find she was gone. And when I questioned Latravis on the matter, he laughed and said he'd seen to the matter —that *the little fledging would be an issue no more*. The seers had been clear and set when they told me the child was born for me, that she was my chosen one. I tried to see to it she was cared for and raised near me so I could protect her always, but I failed her." His throat tightened. "The minute I was gone, I thought my brother had her driven through with a sword."

Gardelle took a seat next to Lazar. "I believe he would have. While on a scouting mission for Kabril, I spotted Sabrina playing near an opening in the castle."

Lazar's eyes widened. He knew how high the Falco castle battlements were and where Sabrina had to be shooed away from often. "She cannot shift forms.

Should she have fallen, it would have been to her death."

"She did fall, Lazar." Gardelle's every word was careful as if not to lose himself in painful memories. "I stopped my quest for the king and caught the child in midair. She looked up at me with eyes I knew well —eyes identical to my sister's. I felt it then, the connection to my family line." He grinned, but it was crooked due to the scar. "She stared at me and called me *avunculus* —uncle. You know how our family lines are imprinted upon us at birth. She knew. She knew and she trusted me fully. It was then I knew her to be Brenya's child. When I landed with her, a hag was there, as if knowing I would be as well. I learned long ago to never question the magik of our kind. She told me quickly of a prophecy involving my niece. That Sabrina was born for the rightful king of the Falco, and that she must be guarded from her own kind until the king was ready to claim his throne and his mate."

Lazar's shoulders slumped.

"So, here we are. From the age of

three, I have raised Sabrina among humans, telling her nothing of our kind, fearing if she knew the truth, she would seek to return because, like so many of us, she is curious and feels as though she belongs anywhere but here."

Unable to verbalize his emotions, Lazar put his hand on Gardelle's arm and patted it, nodding.

Gardelle chuckled. "You do not have to thank me. She is my niece, and I love her greatly. Keep in mind that I raised her believing the hag to be wrong—that there was no son older than Latravis and that Sabrina had no true mate." He stiffened. "You'll not think to be taking her from me on this night. You are nowhere near ready to lead anyone, let alone a woman."

Lazar opened his mouth to protest.

"Was that not you I spotted, *again*, in the buttery, fucking two of the kitchen wenches just yesterday? Your prowess is well-known in the castle. It is said you have had almost *all* of the help since you arrived and that you frequent the beds of the village whorehouse often enough." He gritted his teeth. "I'll not have that around my niece. She deserves better. A man who desires her and her alone. Not one who fucks anything that moves."

While his words were harsh, they were also true. Lazar had taken to craving inter-course several times a day, as if he were trying to fill a void that refused to have anything in it.

Not anything.

Anything but Sabrina.

Drawing in a sharp breath, he ran his hands through his blond hair. His chin sank to his chest, a sure sign of defeat. "I am a man without my people, without a title, without anything but myself to offer Sabrina, and even *that* I have offered to every whore I have come across."

Gardelle said nothing to contradict him.

"I will go," he said, standing, preparing to take flight.

Gardelle rose to his feet, regarding Lazar with hauteur. "Do you do that often?"

"Do what?" He paused with a long,

searching stare placed firmly upon Gardelle.

Stiffening haughtily, Gardelle returned the look. "Run the moment things become too much for you to bear? I mean, you reside in our kingdom now because you ran from your problems in your own, or am I wrong?"

Yes and no.

"Now you run from a female who is but chest high. Perhaps you should go. I want not for my niece to be mated to a coward."

Anger seeped through Lazar's pores. His mouth contorted with rage. He lunged at Gardelle, his intention to inflict as much damage as possible.

The warrior sidestepped him, taking a stance that screamed superiority. Sadly, in this instance he did have the upper hand.

"You are almost too easy to bait, Lazar. Learn to control your temper, or Latravis will use it against you." Gardelle extended a hand of friendship to Lazar. "Come. I believe it is time my niece met my old, dear, trusted friend from Eastern Europe."

"From where?"

"Far from here. Go with me on this. Your accent is thick enough to assure she'll never believe you're a local. While you may enjoy the human realm, you are certainly not from it."

Lazar was confused but shook the man's hand all the same. He hesitated. "Gardelle, there is something you should know."

"More than you are the half-brother to the crazed king of the enemy and mate to my niece?" he questioned with a sardonic grin.

Lazar considered leaving it at that but took a deep breath and told him the truth. "I have dreamed of Sabrina for nearly five years. Of exactly how she is now."

Gardelle's grip on Lazar's hand bordered on too tight. "Dreamed of her how? Visions?"

He licked his lips. There were many details—too many to count—that Lazar felt were left best unsaid in regards to how he'd dreamed of Sabrina. "You might say that, yes." He wisely pried his hand from Gardelle's grip.

The warrior's gaze narrowed in suspicion. "These dreams are not appropriate to speak of with me, her uncle, are they?"

"No." Lazar prepared to be attacked. Gardelle would be within his rights as only kin to Sabrina and her guardian.

Exercising amazing restraint, Gardelle remained in place. "I believe she has dreamed of you as well. Though she has never told me details of her dreams."

Lazar grimaced. If she really had shared dreams with him, then it was best she not tell her uncle. "When I caught her and spoke to her, she said she knew my voice."

"She would, wouldn't she? From when she was little."

Lazar hadn't thought of that. He nodded. "I thought perhaps the legends of mates dream sharing were true."

With a tilt of his head, Gardelle put a hand on his hip, seeming to ponder the idea. "Mayhap they are."

"Gardelle?" Sabrina's voice cut

through the darkness. "Did you find a giant birdman yet? I'm going to make some tea. Want a cup, or would you rather keep hunting mythical creatures? Oo, if you find Bigfoot, be sure to call me. I want to meet him. Better yet, anyone with wings? Bring 'em in, okay, and tell him that I want to be taken flying straightaway, got it?"

Lazar hid his smile. If she only knew.

Gardelle laughed, but it sounded somewhat forced. "Coming, Brina!" He motioned to Lazar. "You and I have some things to discuss, and you will require proper clothing. As you well know, humans do not run about in loincloths."

Lazar flew behind Gardelle through a large open window. He landed in what he assumed to be Gardelle's bedchamber.

Gardelle motioned to the wardrobe there. "Find something to wear, and we shall fly down and enter the home the way humans do—through the back door. I've worked hard assuring my niece knows nothing of our kind. I'll not have that ruined just yet. She will need time enough to accept all that will be laid before her. Throwing it all upon her lap on this night will not occur. Am I clear?"

"Of course." Seemed a waste of time, but Lazar wanted to meet Sabrina and would go to whatever length Gardelle deemed necessary.

Chapter Four

Sabrina exited the expansive kitchen as she heard her uncle coming in the back door. He rarely used the front, which she found to be yet another oddity to pin to Gardelle. She stepped into the hallway. Her uncle wasn't alone. She froze at the sight of the man with him.

Her jaw dropped.

It was him.

The man from her dreams.

The one with the wings.

The one she was positive was her dream lover.

The man followed her uncle deeper into the mudroom. His chin-length, sandy-blond hair looked slightly windblown. His burnt-umber gaze bore into her, and she had to put a hand on the wall to stay upright.

Whoa. That is a lot of man meat.

She jerked, surprised by her rush of hormones and obvious signs of being influenced by her best friend Lisa. It was Lisa who thought of men as objects to be drooled over when need be. Not Sabrina. Not until now.

"Brina," Gardelle said, his tone amused. "A friend of mine has stopped past. Since you're up, I thought you might enjoy it if he joined us for tea."

She opened and closed her mouth several times. What could she possibly say? She could barely think, let alone form a response.

"Something the matter?" her uncle asked.

"Him," she muttered, pointing to the newcomer. All actual intelligent thought process seemed to stop working at the same time. Yes, the man certainly had a way of sending her into hormone over-drive. If she wasn't careful, she'd hear the

telltale sound of her biological clock begin-
ning to tick. Man meat wasn't to be taken
lightly, that much was for sure. "He's the
guy with wings."

Gardelle huffed. "Ah, right. Wings.
Aha. You do realize you were just dreaming, right?"

Yes. That didn't take from the fact the
very man she'd dreamt of catching her was
now standing in the mudroom, staring at
her while he looked like sex on a stick.

"Brina, this is Lazar," Gardelle said, as
if it were no big deal her dream lover was
corporeal. "He's an old friend of mine. I
phoned him earlier, telling him to stop past
regardless the time. It's so rare that he's in
the States that I didn't want to chance not
seeing him. He'll stay with us a bit. I'm
sure you understand."

"In the States?" she asked, finally
getting something that resembled sane and
coherent to fall from her lips. She was just
happy it wasn't the words man meat.

"He's from a small village in Eastern
Europe," Gardelle stressed, as if that
answer alone should stand on its merit. He

had to know better. "You wouldn't know it. It's near the one I was born and raised in."

Lazar inclined his head, his gaze still locked firmly upon her. "Pleasure to meet you."

She nearly swooned at the sound of his voice. Sexy. Rich. Deep. Tinted with an accent she couldn't quite place yet was familiar to her. It was similar to her uncle's and very close to someone else she knew.

Latravis.

She stiffened. Fainting was not an option. In her dreams maybe, but in real life. No. Absolutely not.

Her hormones kept stoking the fire inside her, and she actually fanned herself with her hand just to keep from actually falling over.

Darn that man meat.

"Brina." Gardelle eyed her attire. "I'll show Lazar to the sitting room while you go change into something more fitting company."

She glanced down at herself and groaned. "I'd meet him in my nightgown.

Perfect. Night keeps getting better and better."

She winced, realizing she'd spoken out loud.

Grr, stupid man meat!

Her uncle's laughter echoed behind her as she turned and raced upstairs, changing quickly. The dress she selected came to mid-thigh. It had a high-banded waist, just under her breasts. It was a throwback to the sixties and one of her favorites. She didn't want to be rude and spend hours primping, so she wrapped her hair in a loose bun and tossed some clear lip gloss on before grabbing a pair of sandals and heading back down the stairs.

She went straight to the kitchen, and the kettle began to whistle. She removed it from the burner and set about preparing a tray to serve tea on. It was heavy and awkward to carry. She entered the sitting room, as her uncle called it, and Lazar's attention moved to her. He stood from his seat and came at her, putting his hands out.

"Here. Let me help," he said, moving even closer.

His hands skimmed hers as he took the tray from her. Heat flared up her arms from his touch, and she was pretty sure she'd simply ignite soon. Body temperatures were not meant to run as high as hers currently was. Was it possible to have man-meat heat stroke? She didn't want to lose contact with him, but she didn't want to pass out either.

Never a great way to impress a sexy guy.

"Where would you like it?" he asked.

She motioned to the coffee table, but actually considered motioning to another room—anywhere that would put more distance between them and fast. He was simply too much man for her. "There, please."

He nodded and waited for her to accompany him before doing as asked.

"Thank you." She bent to prepare cups of tea for her uncle and his visitor. She nearly spilled everything because she couldn't seem to pull her gaze from the newcomer. He was breathtakingly hand-some. His face was cut from stone, the edges hard, yet there was a softness in his eyes that was welcoming and mysterious. She could get lost for hours in his dark gaze if permitted.

Lazar.

The name was as intriguing as the man. She wanted to blurt out she'd dreamt of him, and that he'd not only caught her and had wings, but she was pretty darn sure he was her dream lover as well. Wisely, she held her tongue.

She took a seat across from him, next to her uncle. Crossing her legs, she smoothed a hand over her dress and bare thigh. Lazar seemed glued to the action as if it were soft-core porn, watching her hand with an intensity that made her gulp.

If Lisa could see me now, she'd die laughing. Or coach me on how to be a sex kitten.

Gardelle cleared his throat, and she slid closer to him on the sofa. He felt safe. Lazar felt dangerous in a way that could be both good and bad.

"So," she mumbled, her body heating

quickly with each stolen glance she took of Lazar. Men were not supposed to look that good, and they certainly weren't supposed to be dreamworthy. "The two of you are old friends?"

"Yes," said Gardelle.

"But you've never mentioned him before," she protested.

Her uncle cast her a dubious look. "Brina, you talk so much it's difficult for me to get a word in edgewise. How can I be expected to mention everyone I know when you jabber on and on endlessly?"

Nervously giggling, she nodded. Her uncle had an odd sense of humor. One she'd learned to understand when just a child. She knew he was joking. "Uh-huh. Sure."

Lazar set his tea aside and leaned forward, watching her closely, his gaze compelling. "What is it someone your age enjoys doing, Sabrina?"

She stiffened at the sound of her full name. "You mean what do people our age do for fun around here?"

Her uncle and Lazar shared a knowing

look before Lazar inclined his head. It was as if they were having a full conversation yet saying nothing. Strange, but then again so was Gardelle. Stood to reason his friends would be slightly odd too.

Sabrina offered a blasé shrug. "Not much. There are a few bars in town that we sometimes frequent on weekends. The city, about a half hour from here, has better ones and nightclubs. It also has restaurants that aren't too bad. Every now and then a good play or show will come through there."

The edges of his mouth drew upwards. "Today is Friday. That is a weekend, yes?"

"If you're trying to get my niece to drag you to a bar, you're—"

Sabrina cut off her uncle, knowing he'd simply go on and on. "I'd love to take your friend with me tomorrow night— erm, if he's still in town and wants to go. It's a bit late for me to want to head out on the town tonight."

"The night has only just begun," Lazar said steadfastly.

Gardelle grumbled something

inaudible under his breath. It didn't sound friendly or kind.

Ignoring the grump that was her uncle, Sabrina smiled at Lazar. "You sound like Lisa."

"Lisa?" Lazar questioned as her uncle groaned.

"She-devil," Gardelle spat. "Temptress who knows no bounds. Puts terrible ideas into sweet Brina's head."

Sabrina's tongue darted out and over her lip. "Sweet?"

Gardelle eyed her. "As in comparison to that…that…"

She tried to keep from laughing. "She-devil?"

Her uncle gave a curt nod. "Precisely."

"I, for one, would love to meet this Lisa," Lazar said from the sidelines. "For any woman who can cause such a stir in one like Gardelle is worth meeting."

Sabrina grinned. Lisa would more than likely eat both men alive. She wouldn't be at a loss for the right words as was Sabrina. No. Lisa always knew what to say—even if it meant she said too much.

"She's not as bad as he makes her out to be."

"She grabbed my backside last time she was here," her uncle stated, appearing as traumatized by the incident now as he had been when it occurred. "And she held it!"

Sabrina had to lower her gaze to keep from tearing up with laughter. Lazar, however, had no issues with laughing at her uncle's shock. Lazar inclined his head at her. "This nightclub. You would be willing to attend with me tomorrow evening?"

"Sure." She looked at Gardelle. "You should come too, Gardelle. No one ever believes you're old enough to be my uncle or that you're old enough to have raised me. You don't look a day over thirty. I'm sure the ladies would love it if you came too."

Gardelle sighed. "Brina, it is far from my scene."

"So stuffy," she said out of the side of her mouth. "Stodgy."

He laughed. "Yes, well, if your friend

Lisa is also accompanying you, then I most certainly will be too stodgy to attend. She makes me feel as if I'm rare meat and she the hungry lioness."

Sabrina tipped her head back and snorted. She put a hand on her uncle's forearm. "You're still afraid she'll try to kiss you again. I told you once before that she was drunk. She doesn't remember doing it."

His eyes widened. "I spent four hours prying the young female off me. I would remove her, and she would pounce upon me again—like she was the hunter and I the prey. Oh, she is no *mere mortal*. She is a vixen to be avoided at all costs."

Sabrina laughed. Gardelle and his aversion to Lisa was notorious and a serious point of many longstanding jokes between them. She slapped her leg in an unladylike way. "No mere mortal. I can't wait to tell her you said that."

Her uncle chortled. "I'm sure she'll enjoy knowing she's managed to strike fear into one such as me."

Snickering, Lazar pulled her attention

to him once more. "Enough about my friends," she said. "Let's talk about yours, uncle."

Lazar straightened somewhat in the chair. Not many would enjoy being on the spot, but he seemed even more put off by the idea than most.

Interesting.

"And what would you like to know about him?" Gardelle questioned, an odd tone to his voice. "Perhaps if he's single?"

Her head whipped to her uncle. "Excuse me, what?"

With limited success, he attempted to hide his smile. "Just forming a guess as to what you may wish to know of my *friend*."

"All I have so far is that you two go way back and that he's from Eastern Europe. Though his accent isn't one I can place." She shrugged. "I don't claim to know everything about everywhere. So, Lazar, what is it you do for a living?"

Gardelle interrupted as something akin to panic raced over Lazar's face. "He's in private security. Deals with very high-profile clients and of course is contractually bound not to discuss them or matters pertaining to them. You understand, I'm sure."

"Neat," she said, resisting the urge to ask what famous people he might have guarded. Her uncle would shut her down, just as he'd done. It was his way, and regardless what others thought, she loved him despite his flaws. "Do you carry a gun?"

Gardelle grunted. "Brina, really?"

"It's a valid question," she defended, sipping her tea. Man meat with a weapon was one hot image to conjure. "I didn't ask if he's ever killed anyone."

"And you're not going to either," her uncle scolded as if she were a child.

Lazar crossed an ankle over his leg and leaned back in the chair, his muscled body tugging at his clothing. Her mouth watered. She'd dreamed of him minus the clothing and knew every inch of him.

No. You don't. It was dreams. Not real.

Her pulse quickened as she thought back to the countless times she'd dreamt of him. Of being brought to culmination by his gifted hands, mouth and body.

Sabrina had to focus to control her breathing.

Lazar inclined his head. "I generally carry a weapon, but I've no weapon on me now. I like to think I am a walking weapon."

She couldn't help but smile. The man seemed to get sexier by the second. Something that should be against the law. "Double neat."

"Double neat?" Gardelle challenged. "You had the finest education money could buy, and double neat is what you come up with in response?"

She tried not to laugh. It didn't work. "Stodgy."

He smiled as well. "I just want you to make a nice first impression. That is all. I know how incredibly sweet and perfect you are. I'd like Lazar to realize as much as well."

Narrowing her gaze, she eyed her uncle. "Why?"

He merely grinned in response.

Her expression fell as she realized what was happening. "Oh no you didn't."

"I didn't what?" he asked.

"Tell me you did not lose your mind again about how much danger I'm supposedly in and go and hire a bodyguard for me?"

"Relax," he said quickly. "Lazar is not here because I hired him to protect you. He is as I said, an old friend. You can stand down now, small one."

"You know," she said absently. "I'm actually tall for a girl. I can't help that you're a giant and apparently so are all your friends."

Lazar chuckled. "He has a point, Sabrina. You are quite tiny, at least in comparison to us and the women we're used to."

She glanced nervously at him and pushed the stray strands of her hair behind her ears. "I, um, prefer Brina. Hearing you say my whole name is…"

"Strange," Gardelle offered.

"No. Familiar," she admitted, and then regretted it.

"Really?" Lazar asked, his fingers easing along the edges of the oversized chair. "As if I have maybe said it before in a dream or maybe the past? When you were young?"

She stiffened at the mention of dreaming. Had he shared the same dreams?

Blushing from head to toe, she thought of what they'd done in her dreams. Things she'd never actually done in real life. In fact, in real life she was far from experienced. She laughed nervously, and then it faded as she found herself thinking more about what he'd said—about the past. He was right. That wasn't possible though. He didn't look any older than she. Thinking herself mad, she snorted. "I know what it is. It's the name—Lazar. It reminds of when I was little. I had this imaginary friend, and your name makes me think of what I named him. That must be it."

Gardelle's entire posture changed. He stared at her, and an odd dawning seemed to come over him. "Zar-Zar."

She smiled wide. "You remember."

"I do," Gardelle responded, his gaze

sliding to Lazar. "She asked for *him* until she was nearly seven."

Sabrina set her cup on the table. "It's been a long time, but I have fuzzy—limited memories of then."

"Do you remember crying for him?" Gardelle asked cautiously. "Telling me he was sad and that he missed you?"

She shook her head. "Nope. I had a very vivid imagination, so who knows what I came up with. I do know that I was positive he had wings and could fly. Crazy. I know. I must have a thing for wings."

Lazar choked on his tea. He coughed before setting it down. "Yeah. Crazy."

"I think I just gave your friend the impression I'm a nutjob," she said to her uncle.

Lazar perked. "No. Not at all. I'm curious about this imaginary friend of yours. The one with the wings. Do you remember anything about him?"

She thought about changing the subject but decided there was no harm in answering. "He was safe. Whenever I dreamed him up, I felt totally and completely safe. When he was gone, I was terrified. I don't remember of what or who or even why. My first full memories aren't until I'm around four or so and I was already living with Gardelle by then. I do know that I couldn't see my imaginary friend anymore. I remember drawing him pictures and telling him stories about my day even though he wasn't there." She snorted. "Not that he ever was, but you get what I'm saying."

"You used to ask for him for Christmas and your birthdays," Gardelle stated. "I never realized he was real."

"Real? No," she said. "He felt real to me when I was little but then again so did the boogeyman. If we could stop focusing on me and my lame childhood delusions, that would be great."

Gardelle touched her arm. "Refresh my memory again, Brina. You were seven when you stopped asking for Zar-Zar. It was about the same time your pet came into your life, yes?"

"Yep."

Lazar tipped his head. "A pet?"

"Yes. Brina was playing outside, near the creek, when her screams alerted me to a problem. I ran to find her on her knees next to an injured domestic falcon."

Sabrina sighed at the thought. "He was cute and helpless. And you wanted to shoot him and put him out of his misery."

Her uncle shifted uncomfortably. "I have apologized numerous times for that."

"I can't believe you would actually shoot a poor, innocent, defenseless bird. And don't try that ending-his-suffering bit again. It didn't work on me when I was seven, it won't work now," she said.

He grunted. "I know. You insisted he be brought into the house and tended to. He was most displeased with the idea of me lifting him."

"Yeah, you wanted to shoot him," she replied. "That would turn me off to you too."

Lazar chuckled.

"But you," her uncle stressed. "You, he permitted to pick him up without any issue."

She rolled her eyes. "Because my first response wasn't to shoot him."

Gardelle laughed, but it lacked a smile that reached his eyes. "Brina, you dismiss your way with him and joke it off when we both know you formed a bond with him. He was born in the wild and had lived a free life before you. After you cared for him, he refused to return to the wild."

"Not true," she said, taking slight offense. "He totally lived outside."

"He went no farther than required to hunt for food and returned to the tree outside your bedroom window. There is where he made his home until his passing."

"Can we stop talking about Prince?"

"Prince?" Lazar questioned.

She nodded. "Yes. I named the falcon Prince."

"Prince what?" asked Gardelle.

She bit her lower lip. "Prince Zar."

He shot Lazar a knowing look.

Lazar seemed elated by the news. "You're a very interesting young woman."

"Thanks. I think."

Chapter Five

GARDELLE SAT, HIS BODY TENSE AS HE broke bread with a man he'd never truly believed existed. He'd become so overprotective of Sabrina that having her destined mate here in his home made him contemplate running Lazar through with a sword. Sadly, he'd come to know Lazar over the course of his stay within the Kingdom of the Hawks. He was a good man. A much better man than his brother, King of the Falcons.

Latravis's cruelties knew no bounds. His own kind lived in fear of the mad king who ruled their lands. None challenged the throne from within. They obeyed because the alternative was death. The kingdoms surrounding that of the Falcons had lived centuries dealing with the madness that leaked out. Wars ravished the borderlands, and hate was deeply ingrained on both sides. Theirs weren't the only warring kingdoms in Accipitridae. The Eagles had a longstanding feud with the Vultures, and the Buzzards made life for the Osprey difficult while still managing to feud with most of the realm. The Owls were the only ones who seemed to have cooler temperaments and less war. They were often called in during times of peace negotiations. Though they were not to be dismissed when war was needed. They could be fierce when called for.

Latravis had managed to isolate his kingdom from not only the Hawks but, at last check, all, including the Owls, were now in alignment against him. That was saying something. Getting the rest of the kingdoms to lay down arms against each other long enough to take them up against you spoke volumes to your lack of character.

Gardelle sighed. Sabrina would be

drawn into their world even though he'd sought to keep it from her. There was nothing he could do to stop it. Her mate was truly alive and here, sitting before her, looking as if he was barely containing the need to touch her.

This wasn't what he wanted for his niece, but not much that had happened in her life had been what he'd have picked. Lazar could mean happiness, a family, immortality. He could also be the bringer of death should his brother come into play.

ACCIPITRIDAE REALM in the Kingdom of the Falcons, on the borders of Falconidae...

"MY LORD," Ennae, a trusted member of the guards, said as he approached the throne. His walk was slow down the long, narrow center of the throne room.

Latravis tapped the edges of the chair

and lifted a hand, beckoning the warrior closer. "What is it?"

"The bastard," stated Ennae through gritted teeth.

"What has he done now? Defected to the *Kestrels* now?" The traitor had left the service of his king to bow down to the king of their enemy—the Hawks. Kabril and his fellow Hawks were weak. They had somehow been lucky enough to hold off Latravis's attacks, but they were no match for him—for his armies. He'd see all the Hawks dead or in chains before the end of his lifetime.

Ennae eyed Latravis warily. "He is within the human realm. To the east, and within one day's flying distance from the nearest portal, if my information is correct."

With a shrug, Latravis cast an unimpressed look toward his guard. "This matters to me how? He often whores around there, yes? Yet none of you have been able to find and kill him as I ordered."

"We have his scent. He was not careful to mask it this time."

Latravis grinned. "Interesting. See to it he's tracked. Find what holds his interest and report back to me. Perhaps a trap can be laid for the bastard. It is high time he was dealt with. I'll not have him threaten my crown again."

"Of course not, my lord," Ennae said. "You are the one true king."

A sick smile danced upon Latravis's face. "I am. And all shall bow down to me. This realm will be mine."

A flicker of doubt crossed Ennae's face, and Latravis considered having the man's head removed. He decided against it. To date, Ennae had been loyal. "See to it the bastard is tracked and a trap is laid."

"Yes, my lord." Ennac exited the throne room with quick strides.

Latravis shook his head, pain piercing his temple as he struggled through the darkness and insanity that had become his life. Reason crept in. *To the east. Within one day's flying distance.*

Too close to Sabrina for his liking.

He held on to reason and sanity long enough to stare down at his hands. Hands that had taken too many lives to count since the great bird sickness had come over him centuries ago. He knew once the madness returned it would try to seek out Sabrina or send others to do so, and he knew in the end she could be harmed should he lose control.

He'd always known what a threat he could be to her. It was why he'd seen to it she could protect herself should the time ever come that she be forced to do so— even if it was against him.

His sane moments, few and far between, were filled with worry and dread over what may come to pass.

She was light. She was salvation. She was not to be harmed if he could help it. Unfortunately, the *him* of now was rarely in charge anymore. The mad version was who issued the orders and the mad version was nearly fully in control. Only the most trusted of his men knew of Sabrina's existence. Ennae was not one. He would view the female as a weakness, especially if he saw how lucid she made Latravis.

———

SEVERAL AWKWARD, silent moments passed before Gardelle and Lazar began having a conversation Sabrina couldn't follow. It didn't matter. Her concentration was on Lazar and how good-looking he was. She actually welcomed the opportunity to simply stare for a bit. He had a face one would never tire of.

Her uncle nudged her. "Brina?"

"What?" she asked, snapping to attention.

He laughed. "Have you heard a word Lazar was saying to you?"

"Um." Pink stole her cheeks.

"You were staring intently at him. I assumed you were listening to him," Gardelle stated.

"No. I was pretty much just staring at his lips." Groaning, she blushed more. "More tea?"

No takers.

Of course.

Gardelle nudged her again. "His lips? Dare I ask?"

"Please don't," she begged, wanting off the subject.

Lazar's mouth tugged upward, only adding to his appeal. She forced her gaze to the window and off him. It was a case of do that or risk leaping upon the man.

There was a pounding at the front door. Gardelle and Lazar stood fast, looking as though they were ready for an attack.

"Sabrina," a female voice called. "Your lazy butt better not be back in bed. So help me God I will drag you out of it by your hair."

Gardelle groaned. "What is she doing here?"

Sabrina shrugged and stood as well. "It's Lisa. Does she need a reason? I'm pretty sure 'unpredictable' is her middle name." She cast a worried glance at Lazar, already knowing her friend would try to sink her claws into the man.

With her head held high, Sabrina went

out to the front entranceway. She opened the door just as the sassy blonde began pounding upon it once more. Lisa, as usual, was dressed in skintight clothing that showed off her voluptuous figure. She always seemed to exude sex. Sabrina wasn't sure how and secretly wished she had the ability. Next to Lisa she looked as stodgy as her uncle.

Lisa stopped and looked her up and down. "Goodie, you're almost ready."

"Ready for what?" Sabrina tried to keep the door open a crack in order to block Lisa's view of the sitting room and mainly Lazar.

"To go out." Lisa pushed past Sabrina. "I'm not a fan of the dress, but I'm used to you and know the odds of me getting you into leather pants or a leather skirt are about the same as me hitting the lottery."

"Lisa, I'm not going out tonight. It's late."

Lisa burst into laughter. "It's eight thirty. What are you, ninety-five? Live a little, Brina. Let's be young, have fun, screw our way through endless hot guys."

Sabrina blushed from her toes to her head. "Lisa."

"You are so repressed," Lisa said with a snort, heading toward the kitchen. "Too bad your uncle isn't home. I love staring at his ass."

Putting her hand over her eyes, Sabrina attempted to will herself away. It didn't work. When Lisa grew silent, she knew her friend had spotted the men.

"Yummy," whispered Lisa. That was code for Lisa had her sights on them and odds were would try to get one of them into bed. Lisa had actually coined their best-friend tag of man meat. And she'd certainly find Lazar worthy of the title.

Sabrina was put off by the idea anyone would find her uncle attractive that way because he was her family. The thought Lisa would make a play for Lazar set Sabrina's teeth on edge, causing her to grind her molars.

Sabrina hurried toward Lisa, trying to steer her in the direction of the kitchen. Lisa stared unabashedly into the sitting room. "How is it possible to have that much man meat in one area?"

"If I beg, will you not speak?" Sabrina asked, ever hopeful it might work.

Lisa snickered. "I'll not speak if you agree to go out partying with me tonight."

Gardelle cleared his throat, a disapproving note to the act. It also meant he and Lazar could hear everything Lisa had been saying.

"Oh, lighten up," Lisa said to him. "She's way legal and can come and go as she pleases. You worry way too much."

Sabrina touched Lisa's arm. "Remember the talk we had?"

"Which one?"

"The one about you and your lack of filters?" Sabrina stared harder at her friend.

"Oh, that one," Lisa said. "Yes. What? Am I saying the first thing that comes to mind again?"

"And then some."

Lisa pursed her lips. "Sorry."

"Kitchen. *Please*."

"Can I just say one more thing?" Lisa

didn't wait for an answer. "Who is the hottie?"

Gardelle's hands clenched. "Lisa, meet my friend Lazar."

"Lazar?" Lisa smiled from ear to ear as she swayed her hips, heading right into the sitting room and for Lazar. She put her hand out to him. "My, my, aren't you a looker?"

Sabrina saw green as Lazar kissed Lisa's hand. She quickly quelled her jealousy. "Lisa, let's go to the kitchen and talk there. We can let my uncle and his friend catch up alone."

"Oh, honey, you cannot possibly want to be out of this room." Lisa paused and tipped her head, staring at Lazar. "He looks really familiar. I know. The eyes and hair. Latravis has the same ones. Same build too, but not quite as big as Lazar. Close though."

Gardelle and Lazar stiffened, both men looking to Sabrina.

"Latravis?" Gardelle asked, a curious yet angry note to his voice.

"Lisa, how about you help me get my

hair and makeup done? I'd love to go out with you." Sabrina wanted away from the subject and fast. If giving in to Lisa's demands to go out would do the trick, she was game.

Lisa, clueless to what was going on, shrugged and smiled. "Yeah. Latravis is this guy who shows up a lot in the same circles we run. Has a thing for Sabrina. Big time. Bordering on stalking in my opinion but seems harmless enough. Sexy. Very sexy."

Lazar's expression changed.

Gardelle looked horrified. "This Latravis only just began running in the same circles?"

Lisa waved a hand dismissively. "Pfft. No. He's been lingering for years now. He doesn't really speak much to me. Acts likes he's too good to be bothered or something. But he tries *very* hard to catch and keep Sabrina's attention." She shook her head at Sabrina. "Honey, the man screams money. I don't know why you don't give in and date him. He showers you with gifts. And talk about surrounding himself with man meat. Those guys who are always with him are hot."

Gardelle undid his top shirt button. Sabrina knew he was pissed and trying not to blow up in front of Lisa. "He showers you with gifts?"

"He tries to," Lisa said. "Brina doesn't accept them. Doesn't mean the man stops trying. Even calls her his queen."

Lazar's entire body tensed, and he looked lethal.

So did her uncle.

Gardelle met her gaze. "His queen?"

Lisa chomped her gum and kept digging Sabrina into a bigger hole with her uncle. "Yeah. Makes these weird comments about some gods or something getting it all wrong and that she should be with him instead. It's creepy in one respect but way romantic in another. I don't know why Sabrina holds out on him and doesn't give in to his advances. I'd be so open to rich, hot and horny."

Sabrina squeaked, wanting desperately to fade away.

"Strange how Brina has never once

mentioned this suitor to me," Gardelle said, anger evident on his face.

"Not really," Lisa replied. "You treat her like she's ten sometimes, so she tries her best to minimize upsetting you in any way. I know your thoughts on her and dating any man, so I'm not shocked in the least she'd keep Latravis a secret."

"Lisa," Sabrina scolded.

"What? It's true. He's barely home anymore, and you still obey almost all the rules he gave you when you were a teenager. It's kind of sad. I've been telling you for years to move out and get a place of your own. You're going to be twenty-four soon, Brina. I get that you love the guy and have this huge amount of guilt because he's raised you since you were little and your parents died, but that doesn't mean you have to spend the rest of your life with him—letting him act like a warden."

She glanced at Gardelle and offered an apologetic look. "I don't think of you like a warden. And I like living here—with you. I don't want to move away just yet.

Unless…" She bit her lower lip. "…you want me to."

"Most certainly not," Gardelle snapped. "You are an unmated young female. To permit you to live on your own is too much, even for me. Already I've given you more freedoms than other women, and it is clear you have abused those."

Sabrina hung her head in shame. Keeping Latravis from him was a mistake, but she'd honestly thought it was a harmless one. Latravis had always been overprotective of her. In fact, he'd gone above and beyond on more than one occasion to make sure she was safe. Arguing the fact with her uncle was pointless. When it came to Latravis, there was no reasoning with him. Things were very black and white in regard to Latravis—at least according to her uncle.

"Hold on one minute there," Lisa argued in her defense. "Unmated female? What does that even mean? Are you trying to say that because she's not married off to some man that she's incapable of thinking on her own or living on her own? And you've given her too much freedom as is? You have got to be kidding me. Who are these women you know, and are they from the Stone Age?"

"Lisa," Sabrina pressed apprehensively.

"Grow a backbone with him, Brina," her friend advised. "You have one with everyone else in your life. Everyone but your uncle. You worry nonstop about him when he's off on his seemingly endless business trips, and I can see the guilt in your eyes when you're out at a place you know he'd disapprove of. Stop acting like a child, and stop acting like he's your father. He's some loaded rich uncle who took you in. He's barely been around enough to qualify as anything more."

Gardelle took a step back.

Lisa advanced on him. She was hardly the type of woman to back down, unlike Sabrina who often found more comfort in nodding and remaining silent. "I've known her since she was fifteen. That's nearly ten years, and don't think for one second I haven't noticed how rarely it is you're home or even around."

"When I could not be, and she was young, I assured someone was here to care for her and watch over her," Gardelle stated in a defensive manner, some of the fire leaving his eyes.

Lazar leaned forward more, listening intently. This wasn't the conversation Sabrina wanted to have in front of him, but with as hardheaded as both Gardelle and Lisa were, there was no stopping it.

"Live-in housekeepers don't count as family, Gardelle," Lisa snapped, her temper showing. "My God, the girl spent so many nights in tears, wanting to ask questions about herself and having no one around who could answer them, that I lost count. And don't think I don't know that before the two of you moved here, that it was the same for her. That as far back as she can remember, you've been running off —your job more important than her. Brina would never admit it to you or even herself. She's that nice of a person. So don't you stand there acting like she's let you down so much, when in truth, I'm thinking it's you who let her down."

Gardelle opened his mouth and then closed it before exhaling. "I tried to provide her with everything she could possibly need. She wanted for nothing. She still wants for nothing."

Lisa rolled her eyes. "Like Brina gives a shit about material things. I'm betting you she'd trade everything she has for extra time with you—her *only* anything. In her eyes, you're a father and a mother to her. You're way more than an uncle, but you don't see it. You'd know that had you shown up to one thing she had schoolwise. I can't recall a time you were ever at anything all through high school. And I know when she started college, you were equally as absent for anything important there."

Her uncle gave her a questioning look. He didn't understand what he'd done wrong, and she knew it.

Lisa didn't let up. When she had a bone, she didn't just run with it, she sprinted, buried it and then dug it up to run some more. "Who doesn't even show to their kid's graduation? High school or college? For Christ's sake, she was the damn head of the class and had not one person outside of me there for her to show her support. And she's let you down? Really?"

Gardelle appeared confused. "This graduation, it was something important?"

Lazar seemed equally as lost as to what graduation was.

Lisa tossed her hands in the air. "Were you raised in a cave or something? Of course it was important. Hugely important. So was every awards dinner Brina was honored at. Every science fair she won. All of it. Hearing about her first kiss or about how the other girls ridiculed her to no end because she was so smart and pretty. How they tried to make her life a living hell. How they would do everything they could to try to humiliate her. Or how about when she went to college two of the girl's professors tried to get down her pants. One went as far as to threaten to flunk her if she didn't give him what he wanted—her."

Sabrina sighed, her shoulders slumping in defeat. Everything that she'd kept from him was being laid out before him. Not only that, it had all been spelled out in front of Lazar, a man she was drawn to in ways she couldn't explain and a man she now felt humiliated before.

"Is it any shock she'd keep Latravis and his advances a secret from you? You barely know her," Lisa said snidely. "Come on, Brina. Let's go. You can crash at my place."

Sabrina remained in place, her gaze moving to her uncle. She teared up. "I know you told me to stay away from him. I'm sorry that I didn't tell you the truth about him."

"You're apologizing to him?" Lisa questioned.

She looked to her friend. "Yes. I hurt him by lying to him about Latravis. I get you have no respect for your parents. But I respect Gardelle even if he's had to be gone a lot in my life. Without him, I'd have no one. He took me in when I was little. He didn't have to. In case you missed it, he's a young, single man. I'm sure having an instant family minus the wife to lend a hand wasn't easy for him. I don't think he was really that close with my mother either. I get the sense he only kind of knew her and sort of ended up with no choice but to raise me."

Lisa shook her head. "Doesn't make it right that he's been gone so much and then talks to you like you're a letdown. And what era does the man think it is?"

"He's different. I know that and I actually like that about him. No, I won't lie and say I loved the fact he's rarely around or that a string of nannies raised me, but I'm not going to cry in my milk over it. He's all I have, and I do think of him like a father. He didn't come to anything while I was growing up because he either didn't know about it or because I didn't explain what it was or what it meant to me."

Lisa arched her brows. "Was he really raised in a cave?" She glared at Gardelle, as if daring him to answer.

Sabrina snorted and smiled. She wanted to smooth over the situation. Peacemaker was a role she stepped into with ease and preferred. She didn't like Lisa's hard-as-nails approach to everything in her life. Quite often quiet observation got one further than instantly flying off the handle. "Sometimes I wonder. His upbringing wasn't normal and his ideas on a lot of things are dated, but had I explained everything to him fully, he'd have found a way to be there for me. I just didn't like bothering him. He had enough to worry about, and his job sometimes leaves him so stressed. I wanted home to be a place he didn't have to worry about. That he could just relax."

"Other children were cruel to you?" Gardclle asked, sounding so lost and out of sorts. "You would tell me you enjoyed your day and had lots of friends."

Lazar's jaw set. He looked as if he was ready to take on Sabrina's long-gone cause. It made the situation easier to bear.

Lisa laughed, unconcerned as always with what she said and who she said it around or to. "The girl had me and that's it. I think the rest of them sucked, so I was damn happy she moved here. She was a breath of fresh air, even if she's really weird sometimes."

Sabrina bit her inner cheek.

"Wendy Stilz pisses me off to this day when I think about her putting that dead pigeon in your locker and spray painting *freak* on the front of the locker door." Lisa grinned. "When you hauled off and decked her a good one, yelling at her for hurting a bird, it was so beautiful. Man, I wish I would have recorded that. What a bitch."

Gardelle gasped and looked at her. "They put dead animals in your locker?"

"Yes," she whispered.

"This is common for high school children to do?" he asked, his gaze going to Lazar.

Lazar shrugged. "I know not. Is it?"

Lisa stared at them both like they were nuts. "Uh, no."

"Then why would they do such a thing to Brina?" questioned Gardelle with a sincerity in his voice that could not be missed.

Sabrina tapped her thigh gently. "Because they called me bird girl. I'd feed the pigeons at lunch and sit alone, away from everyone. Wendy knew I liked them, and she hated me for some reason. So, in order to get a rise out of me, she had her boyfriend of the hour kill one and put it in my locker."

"Joke was on that bitch when you knocked her spoiled ass over the lunch table," Lisa supplied proudly. "Such a beautiful moment."

"She shouldn't have hurt the bird. He didn't do anything to her, and I don't care that people call them the rats of the sky. Pigeons have feelings too."

Lisa laughed. "Honey, you're kind of adorable. You know that, right?"

"I broke the girl's nose," Sabrina said with a sigh. She deplored violence yet had so quickly resorted to it in that instance. What had been even stranger was how strong she'd seemed when she'd set her mind to harming Wendy.

"I know. Fabulous, right?"

She snickered, and some of her guilt eased away. "It did feel kind of good. Your dad was a gem when he came to school to smooth things over for me."

"Yeah, a high-priced lawyer that makes the school system quake in their boots is always nice to have at your disposal."

Gardelle took a seat, his hands going to his knees. "I should have been more attentive, Brina. I should have learned the ways and customs better before raising you here. I thought I was doing everything correctly. I tried to instill some of what I was raised to believe as well."

Taking pity on him, she went to her uncle and bent, hugging him around the neck. She kissed his cheek. "I have no complaints. I love you."

He put an arm over hers and his temple to hers. "I left you feeling alone in all of this and then lash out when you do not share with me all that happens in your life. I cannot fault you for keeping the truth of Latravis from me when your need to keep me worry and stress-free has left you keeping much from me over your life."

"Man, he's hard to stay mad at," Lisa said with a snort. "Sexy guy over here even looks a little less like he might blow now. For a minute, it was touch and go."

Lazar had appeared to calm somewhat. Oddly, she found herself going to him as well. She stepped close to him and went as far as to slide her arms around his waist, as if she'd known him for years. The strange heat sensation returned as she made contact with him. She half-expected him to push her away. He wrapped his powerful arms around her and dragged her against his body.

He put his lips to her ear. "Brina, I know you have no reason to believe me or respect my wishes, but your uncle is correct. Latravis is a dangerous man. I am unsure if he has ever shown that side of himself to you, but I can promise you that it is there—lurking just below the surface. If I were to ask you to consider staying away from him, would you?"

It was on the tip of her tongue to say no, but that wasn't what came out. "Yes."

He rubbed her back, keeping his mouth to her ear and continuing to whisper, "He is cruel and sadistic and when pushed too far, he will strike without warning or reason. I have no wish to see you harmed by him. Already I wonder why it is he has not acted—why he has not harmed you. He enjoys games, but even this game would be long for him to play without reward." He tensed.

She put her mouth to his ear, needing to go to her tiptoes in the process. "If you're wondering if I've had sex with him, I haven't."

Lazar's body relaxed, and he kissed her temple. The act should have been totally bizarre. So should holding on to a man she barely knew. It wasn't. It was the exact opposite. Like it was the most normal thing she'd done all day.

"Um, Brina," Lisa interrupted. "When did you get a boyfriend and not tell me?"

She was about to turn and tell her friend that Lazar wasn't her boyfriend, when he reached down and took her hand in his. He then stepped back slightly and looked to Lisa. "Around two hours ago. Is that a problem?"

Lisa smiled wide. "I like you. You know that with her you just have to hop in there and lay claim, or she'll run the other way like a scared little mouse."

For some reason being referred to as a mouse around Lazar seemed very wrong. Like he was made to be a hunter and being prey wasn't something you wanted to be.

He leaned in closer to her. "Fear not, my little mouse. I am full for now."

She gulped and tried to, in fact, run the other way. It didn't work out as planned with him holding her hand and all. Lisa and Lazar laughed.

Gardelle merely smiled at her. He looked between her and Lazar. "I do hope you manage to keep him on the run, Brina. He should have to work for your affections. You are a special young woman, and Lazar should be aware of as much."

"I am," Lazar said thoughtfully, his thumb caressing her inner wrist.

Lisa clapped her hands. "Ohmygod, he's so incredibly perfect for you, Brina. He's like Latravis minus the creepy vibe he sometimes lets off. Oh, and Lazar seems slightly less full of himself too."

Lazar's entire body tensed as he was compared to Latravis.

Sabrina stepped to him, putting her free hand to his chest. Her fingers skimmed his rippled form just like she'd done hundreds of times before in her dreams. "I don't think he's anything like Latravis."

"Honey, have you noticed the eyes? I thought Latravis's were contacts or something. Who would have thought two guys would naturally have eyes that color. And come on, the facial features are even close. Very close. Like brother kind of close. Hair too."

Sabrina stared harder at Lazar. She shook her head. "I'm not seeing it."

"Are you blind?" Lisa demanded.

She kept staring up at Lazar. She

wanted to kiss him, and it took all she had to control her urges. She wasn't the type of girl who threw herself at a man. Ever. "I honestly don't see what you're talking about."

"Geesh, at least admit the same-color-eyes thing is there. Who else do you know with eyes that shade? What do you even call it?"

"Burnt umber," Sabrina said softly. "And, yes, Latravis's are the same shade, but they're very different too."

"How do you mean?" Lisa asked.

Sabrina lost herself for a moment in Lazar's gaze. "There is a certain coldness in Latravis's eyes. Like he's hiding something big. Really big, and there are times you wonder if he's registering the same emotions as everyone else around him. Lazar's eyes have a certain mysterious quality to them. Like he's got a secret too, but like he's just waiting for the right second to tell you. And most importantly, there isn't anything cold about them."

If anything, they made her burn.

"Honey, you've known the guy two

hours and you're analyzing his eyes to that degree?"

Sheepishly, Sabrina grinned. It felt like she'd known him forever and a day. "You're the one who brought it up. Not me. I was pretty much stuck on his lips for the first hour."

Lisa burst into laughter. "I have never seen you behave this way. Normally you're rolling your eyes at all the guys who try to come on to you. And most of the time, you dodge them entirely. This one lays on the charm in a heavy way and you're practically glued to him. Can I be your maid of honor at the wedding? Oh, can I be your kid's godmother?"

That did it.

Sabrina leapt back from Lazar and nearly tripped over her uncle in the process of putting distance between her and Lazar.

Lisa laughed harder. "I will pull for you, Lazar. But looks like you've got your work cut out for you if you are expecting any sort of commitment out of the girl."

Sabrina waited for Lazar to freak too.

He grinned at her, his gaze raking over her slowly. "You will find I can be most patient when called for."

She sat down fast next to her uncle.

Gardelle chuckled and put an arm around her. "Fear not, Brina. I will beat him with a stick should he attempt to whisk you away and claim you for himself before the time is right."

She gasped and looked at her uncle. "Don't you mean at all? You'll beat him period. Like for good. As in, never letting him whisk me away?"

Gardelle's laugh was loud and long. He even teared up. "I sat here worrying that I was too controlling and that I held too tight to you, only to have you now insist I hold tighter. Lazar is a good man, and from the way the ladies speak of him—he is very handsome."

She stilled and lifted a defined brow. "Ladies? How many ladies we talking here, because I have this sinking feeling I'm not going to like the number."

Gardelle patted her shoulder. "I guarantee you will not. But something tells me

Lazar's days of countless women are numbered..." He looked to Lazar. "...if not already over. If I was to guess, I would think only one woman will do for him now."

Lisa approached Lazar and looped her arm through his. "Buddy, that one woman better be my friend, or I'll rip your nuts off and cram them down your throat." She smiled sweetly.

Sabrina sucked in a fast breath.

Lazar offered a sexy smile. "It would appear my body will remain intact."

It took Sabrina a second to catch on to what he was saying. She was the one woman her uncle was referring to.

A tiny squeak came from her.

Lazar winked. "Are you well, little mouse? You look pale."

She pressed tight against her uncle's side.

Gardelle chuckled more. "Continue, Lazar, and your *little mouse* will flee. The hunt may be exciting, but I am guessing she is quicker than you believe her to be."

Lazar appeared to welcome the idea of pursuing her.

She gulped.

Lisa grinned. "Man, I am so enjoying this night. Hey, Gardelle, wanna go make out and give Lazar and Sabrina some time alone?"

It was Gardelle's turn to press against Sabrina. "Do not dare leave her alone with me."

Sabrina laughed. "The *mere mortal* scares the heck out of you, doesn't she?"

"Wanna take me out on the town?" Lisa asked. "It's either do it, or you and me sneak in some alone time."

Gardelle's eyes widened more. "Out. Out is good. Out works."

Chapter Six

THE LIGHTS OF THE CLUB WEREN'T exactly doing much in the way of providing adequate lighting. Sabrina stayed close to Lazar. Lisa had dragged Gardelle out onto the dance floor the moment they arrived and had attempted to do the same to Sabrina. Thankfully, Lazar had saved her, sliding an arm around her waist and tugging her tight to him.

The club scene was Lisa's idea of fun. Sabrina had never completely taken to it. Still, she came all the same, happy to be out of the house.

Lazar held a drink in his free hand but kept his other arm around her. He'd managed to keep her close from the word go. He leaned against the bar, sipping his drink as he pulled her closer. She was left no choice but to lean against him. She didn't mind.

His lips pressed to her ear. "It is very loud here."

It was.

He'd been talking directly into her ear since their arrival. Each time he did, his deep voice reverberated through her. Her entire body was on overdrive this close to him.

She shut her eyes and sank against his embrace. She'd done the very same thing in more than one of her erotic dreams. Her hand went to his, the one on her hip. She considered moving his hand off her and stepping away, but the thought vanished quickly as Lazar's lips skimmed her earlobe. "The music has slowed. We shall dance now."

"No," she protested, but he ignored her. He set his empty glass on the bar and guided her to the dance floor. She caught sight of Lisa through the crowd. Gardelle seemed to have surrendered to the inevitable with her and was dancing near her.

Lazar turned Sabrina to face him. He jerked her closer. She stared at the muscular chest before her. The snug-fitting black T-shirt did nothing to take from just how ripped the guy was—in fact, all it did was outline every rippling muscle and bulge.

Darn man meat.

Gulping, Sabrina forced her gaze higher. Her mouth watered at the size of his neck.

Lazar swayed their bodies to the beat. She danced with him, allowing him to lead. His powerful frame flexed against her, and she couldn't stop the whimper of desire that fell from her lips.

Lazar's hands eased down her back, lower and lower. Finally, they settled on the top of her backside. Sabrina would have normally slapped a man across the face for being so bold. She didn't with him. Instead, she touched his neck, her thumbs caressing his jawline as she stared up at him. He moved with a fluid motion that was almost inhuman, yet totally hypnotic.

Never had she been so fascinated with a man before. Sure, she'd found more than her fair share pleasing on the eyes, but this was different. Carnal.

The slow song ended too soon. A faster song came on. She went to walk away from Lazar, but he held firm to her. He began to move once more, his thigh pushing between her legs. Sabrina rocked with him, countering his semi-thrusts that matched the driving beat of the techno music.

His lips found her ear again as his thigh ground against her mound. Pleasure began to build, and she gripped his forearms as best she could, tipping her head, wanting his lips on her neck. He seemed to read her mind, his mouth sampling the tender skin just behind her ear.

She melted against him.

Shockingly, she made the next move. She turned her head, and their lips touched. Sabrina half-thought he might pull away. He didn't. His tongue darted into her mouth, and she opened to him. Her tongue danced around his, letting him lead just as her body did on the dance floor.

She'd never made out on a dance floor with a man she'd only met a few hours earlier. This was out of character yet felt completely right, as if she should have been doing this with him from the moment they met.

She had to go to her tiptoes to keep her lips locked with his. He bent more, as if sensing her strain. He lifted her like she weighed nothing. She yelped into his mouth, and he chuckled, keeping hold of her. Their tongues locked once more, and she wrapped her arms around his neck. His kisses were familiar. Just as they'd been in her dreams.

She ate at his mouth, eager for more. He gave her what she wanted, and moisture pooled at the apex of her thighs. Startled by her raw need for him, she broke the kiss and panted in his embrace. "Lazar."

He closed his eyes and seemed to compose himself. He didn't set her down though. "My apologies. You are a lady, and I take far too many liberties with you."

She stared into his eyes for the longest time before kissing the tip of his nose. "Find a creative way to shake my uncle and you can take far more with me."

Lazar's expression changed to one of shock. He glanced in the direction she'd last seen her uncle in. He set Sabrina down gently but kept her close. "You have no idea how much I wish to accept what you offer, but, Sabrina, you deserve better."

She bit her lower lip. "That may be so but—"

He dipped his head and kissed her tenderly. When he drew back, her lips stayed puckered for a moment, plump from his kisses. "Know that I want you. More than I've ever wanted any woman, but we'll do this right. Proper."

She wanted to argue with him but couldn't. He was treating her with respect, something every woman wanted. With a pout, she nodded.

He grinned and drew her close, dancing with her again. Song after song went by too fast for her liking. Before Sabrina knew it, the night was over. She didn't want it to be. She wanted to stay forever in his embrace, as strange as that sounded.

EVERY OUNCE of restraint was called for within Lazar. Sabrina was so close, tempting and so willing. Damned be the bird gods. He wasn't what she deserved. She deserved more. Better than him, yet he couldn't fathom walking away from her.

Her tiny frame begged to be protected, loved, sampled for all eternity. Already he'd confirmed her kisses were identical to those he'd dreamed of. Would being in her feel the same?

His cock throbbed with need.

He didn't want proper. He wanted to be balls-deep in her. He wanted to release so much seed in her there was no question she carried his offspring. He wanted more than he had a right to ask from her. He'd lain with so many women. He'd used countless cunts to try to satisfy his manly needs. None worked.

Now, when he finally had the one woman created for him, he felt like a fraud before her. A whore. One who should be king of his people and Sabrina his queen. Now she was simply the mate to the whore traitor.

Chapter Seven

LAZAR, STILL DAMP FROM HIS SHOWER, finished dressing in a different set of clothing Gardelle had provided him with for the new day and headed out of one of the guestrooms just as Lisa was leaving the other. She caught his eye and smiled. While the smile held the temptation of sex, he didn't get the sense she was offering, and even if she was, he wasn't interested. Only Sabrina interested him.

"Morning," she said.

"More like good afternoon," he corrected. They'd returned from the night-club after last call, spent the night deep in conversation about everything yet truly nothing at all and had only retired at the sight of the morning sun rising. It seemed as though the house had slept the day away.

Lisa inhaled. "Mmm, smell that? That's Brina's cooking. I'd know it anywhere. The girl is magik in the kitchen."

She grabbed Lazar's arm and tugged, hurrying down the stairs and in the direction of the kitchen. Lisa came to a grinding halt at the entranceway. She put a finger to her lips and then pointed to Sabrina.

Lazar looked to find his mate busily preparing what seemed to be a feast of sorts. Her long hair was braided and wrapped up tightly, showing off her classically beautiful features. The dress she wore was similar in style to the one she'd had on last night. This one was pale pink and more frilly on the ends than the other. Her legs were left showing, and the very sight of them made him hard. Everything about Sabrina did.

He wanted the feel of her lips upon his once more. Her kisses had chased away his inner demons. They'd filled the void he'd had in his heart for so long.

Music played at a low level, and Sabrina danced her way to the stove. The action made Lazar smile like a lovesick fool. Lisa giggled softly and nodded, still pointing at Sabrina.

Sabrina's ass began to move in exact rhythm with the beat. It was all too easy to picture her above him, riding him with the same hip movements—taking him deep. She danced around the kitchen, preparing the meal, dancing the entire time. Her body was hypnotic. Never had he wanted a woman so. He wanted to rush into the room, toss her onto the counter and bury himself so deep into her that she screamed his name.

He tensed. Since he'd come to live among the hawks, his bed partners for the most part had been hawk females. While they welcomed him willingly into their bodies, they still spoke to him as though he were the enemy. Some spit at him during sex, others clawed at his neck and face, telling him he was filth as they begged him to fuck them harder. He didn't mind. He craved the rough, angry sex. It reaffirmed how he'd felt since he'd become an outcast among his own kind—like a traitor.

He looked longingly at Sabrina, wondering if she too would spit at him, cursing his name as he pleasured her body. When still among the Falcons, he'd had countless lovers in his long lifespan. None really held his interest, and he loved none. They'd not spit and hit at him. They'd tried their best to ensnare him—praying and doing all they could to conceive the impossible. A child.

Had one of them managed, it would have meant he was their mate. The woman would have found herself living a life of luxury. As a royal guard, for any side really, compensation and prestige followed. Even under Kabril's rule, Lazar held a similar position as he had with his own kind. But the hawks didn't view him as one of them yet. Money meant little to him. Respect meant everything to him. Or at least it had until meeting Sabrina.

Unable to stop himself, he stepped into the kitchen, wanting to pull her into his arms and kiss her. She turned, a knife in hand, at the same moment. Gasping, she looked up and let the knife fly at him. Lazar's reflexes were far superior to any human's, yet he found himself narrowly missing taking the knife to the head. It embedded into the wall directly behind him, in the exact spot his head would have been had he not moved quickly.

Sabrina's brown eyes widened and grew moist. She cupped her mouth and then ran at him, tossing her arms out wide as she threw herself against him. "Ohmygod. Ohmygod. I'm so sorry. Ohmygod."

"Nice!" Lisa exclaimed, ever the one to interject nonsense in a serious time. "You've got to teach me that, girlfriend."

Ignoring her friend, Sabrina patted Lazar's body, checking for injury, and he smiled, taking hold of her wrists. She was so close, so perfect and so accessible. As much as he wanted to sample her lips, he knew better than to try. She wasn't one of the whores he'd become accustomed to. She was a woman, a lady who demanded respect.

She's my mate.

He could barely control himself. He lifted her arms, returning them to their position around his neck. He put his hands on her hips. As he bent to whisper to her, he inhaled her sweet scent. His entire body ached to be in her. "You missed."

Barely.

She blinked up at him, and fat tears ran down her cheeks. Lazar dipped his head more and used his mouth to kiss them away. She didn't protest. Instead, she wrapped her arms around his neck tighter, her heart beating madly. "I'm so sorry."

"All is well," he encouraged. His lips brushed hers, and they both stiffened at the act. As Sabrina closed her eyes and tilted her head to one side, Lazar realized she was welcoming a kiss. He went in for it, pleased to know her feelings had not changed come morning light.

Their tongues had only just touched when the kiss was rudely interrupted by Lisa. Her laughter filled the room. "Enough with the lip locking, or just get a room before Gardelle spots you. I played heck with him when he noticed the two of you making out on the dance floor. Man, he is overprotective."

Sabrina teared up again. "I'm so sorry, Lazar."

"Take it easy, Brina," Lisa said. "The guy is fine. You missed him by a long shot."

Lazar wasn't sure what a long shot was in her world, but in his, that was not it. Seasoned warriors threw with less accuracy than he'd witnessed Sabrina doing.

"Someone want to tell me what's going on?" Gardelle asked, entering the room. He arched a brow, his scarred side pulling slightly at the sight of Sabrina in Lazar's arms. "And why, exactly, is there a knife in the wall?"

Sabrina's tears returned, and she cried harder this time.

Lazar lifted her in his arms, her feet dangling. He put his forehead to hers, their noses touching. It was intimate in a way he wasn't used to. "Little mouse, I am fine. Cry no more, or I will be forced to lay you out and kiss every inch of you to chase away your sorrow."

She hiccupped and tensed.

He laughed softly and kissed the tip of her nose. "Something smells delicious." He wagged his brows. "In case you're wondering, it's you. The food is a very close second though."

Gardelle made an odd noise as if choking on nothing but thin air.

Lazar set Sabrina down, and she scurried away, glancing nervously over her shoulder to him and then to the knife in the wall. Lisa moved into action, assisting her best friend and taking Sabrina's focus from the events at hand. The two women began taking food into the dining room.

Once alone with Gardelle, Lazar faced the man.

Gardelle was eying the knife. "She did this?"

He nodded. "I startled her."

"Lucky she's not a better aim," Gardelle said with a slight smile.

Lazar didn't laugh. Shifter males had amazing reflexes, and to narrowly avoid something such as a knife being thrown at them was saying something. "Her aim was excellent. I only just missed taking that to the skull."

Gardelle pried the knife from the wall and stared down at it. "The force she must have thrown this with to embed it as far as it was…"

"She is more like our kind than I believe even you suspected," Lazar said, slight pride welling in him.

"Even our women would not be able to throw a knife in such a way," Gardelle countered. "I can barely think of any of the young male recruits who could do as much. And they have been raised in the ways of knives and weaponry and have centuries under their belts."

"Ah, Gardelle," Lazar said. "You're

forgetting one thing. Sabrina is far from any woman I know. Our kind or not."

Gardelle nodded but seemed lost in thought while looking at the knife. "Do you think someone has trained her? Or do you believe the act purely instinctual?"

Lazar thought upon it. He wasn't sure he liked his response. "A touch of both?"

Gardelle met his gaze. "The only other shifter I am aware of her knowing is Latravis. I do not think he would train her to protect herself, do you?"

Lazar snorted. "No. A woman capable of splitting his skull is not a woman he would wish to have around. I believe he would keep any and all sharp objects from her for fear his personality would gift him a slit throat from her."

"You two coming?" Lisa asked, peeking her head into the kitchen.

Lazar couldn't help but notice the way Gardelle's gaze lingered over the female. For a man who was supposedly terrified to be alone with the vixen, his gaze seemed to say otherwise. It said he was busy undressing her in his mind.

He was an unmated warrior. As far as Lazar knew, Gardelle had never found his life mate, nor did the man seem to take much interest in the opposite sex. Perhaps he did have his sights set upon a female, but for reasons all unto himself, he denied it to all around—possibly even himself.

———

GARDELLE ENTERED the dining room and was surprised at the feast his niece had prepared. She'd taken to cooking at a young age, and he never ceased to be amazed at how well she did it. He noticed the way her gaze slid to Lazar and how her mood lightened as Lazar pulled out a chair for her to sit in. Lazar sat next to her, leaving Gardelle no choice but to sit by the she-devil herself.

Curse the bird gods, she was something all right. Never had he met a woman as forward as she, and he knew some of the most famed whores of the bird realm. Lisa was different. She wasn't a harlot, but she wasn't virginal either. And damn it all if

Gardelle didn't find himself oddly attracted to her.

She was too young for him. He had centuries on her. And she wasn't of his kind and out of the question as a mate. Still, his gaze slid to the tight shirt she wore. It cupped the outline of her ample breasts. Gardelle squeezed his eyes shut as he held the chair out for her.

"My lady," he said with a curt nod.

She sat, her shoulders brushing his fingertips. He sucked in a large breath as his cock responded to her.

She is your niece's best friend, he mentally chastised himself. *And human. Focus.*

He cleared his throat and looked up to find a knowing smile upon Lazar's face. Gardelle thought of getting the knife from the kitchen and finishing what Sabrina had started. He resisted. It took much restraint.

Lisa patted the empty seat next to her. "Come on, big boy, sit by momma."

He gulped.

She laughed.

It was going to be another long evening. He and Lazar would need to head

back to their home realm soon. Gardelle
had perfected the art of being gone long
enough to spend time with his niece
without drawing suspicion in the bird
realm. Lazar's absence would not go unno-
ticed. He was a close friend to Sachin, and
the head of the guards would notice if his
friend was missing for too long.

Gardelle raised a hand, gesturing to all.
"We should eat. Lazar and I will have to
leave soon. He'll be attending a few meet-
ings with me out of town."

Sabrina's smile faltered. "You have to
leave again?"

"I do."

"And he has to go too?" she asked.

It broke Gardelle's heart knowing she
didn't want either of them to go. He
looked to Lazar to find him equally
distraught over Sabrina's obvious
emotional state.

Lazar lifted Sabrina's hand. "Little
mouse, we will not be gone long."

"You'll come back?" Her eyebrows
rose.

Lisa snorted. "I'm guessing you won't

be able to keep him away long. Have you missed the fact the guy sticks to you like glue?"

"I have not missed that," Gardelle said sternly. "I'd rather he stick less to her."

Lisa laughed. "I'm sure *you* would."

Chapter Eight

ACCIPITRIDAE REALM

Lazar stalked through the castle corridors. He didn't want to be there. He wanted to be with Sabrina. Gardelle had convinced him that in order to keep suspicions from rising and any word of him being in her life from reaching Latravis, Lazar needed to be seen doing his normal duties. He hated it.

He didn't want to leave her. He wanted to return to her home and dine with her before sleeping under the same roof as his mate. Gardelle was right. He had to maintain the pretense of normal. There was no telling what Latravis would do should he learn Lazar was now back in Sabrina's life.

One of the kitchen serving wenches stepped into the hall. She stared up at him and offered a seductive smile as she grabbed hold of her bosoms, cupping them so they nearly fell free of her dress. "There you are. I was looking for you."

He tried to step around her, the sight of her no longer stirring his cock as it once had. She planted herself before him and smashed her chest against his.

"The kitchen is empty. I know how much you like to fuck me there." She clawed at his exposed upper chest. "Be a good falcon and do as you're told."

He caught her wrists. "I'm not interested. Find someone else."

She huffed, her eyes growing wide. "Not interested? Since when? How many days ago was it that your prick was in my mouth and then my ass?"

Lazar cringed at the reminder. During it all, it had felt right, like he was chasing away an emptiness. Now it felt as if he'd betrayed Sabrina. He stared down at the wench. "Go from here. I have to report for duty."

Boldly she ripped her wrists free from his grasp and shoved her hand down the front of his loincloth. She grabbed his cock and stroked it. "You want to fuck me. I know you do. You're a dirty traitor, but you can fuck."

He went to yank her hand from his loincloth when Gardelle entered the corridor from the other direction. He came to a grinding halt, his gaze narrowing on Lazar and the wench.

Gardelle was suddenly there, separating Lazar and the woman. Gardelle twisted and punched out, connecting with Lazar's jaw. "You bastard!"

Lazar swayed from the force of the impact. He looked up at Gardelle. "It is not what it appears to be."

"Looked to be like you were getting your cock taken care of by the help!"

The wench sneered. "I can give you release too, if you want it."

Gardelle turned a furious glare on her, and she hurried off. He then faced Lazar. "Stay away from my niece."

Lazar shot forward fast. "The wench grabbed me. I turned down her advances."

"She is the same one I and half the castle have seen you cramming your dick in anywhere you can. The buttery, the kitchen, the dining hall, the hallways," he said, ticking each location off with a finger. "You sicken me. How Brina could be destined for a man with no shame is beyond me."

"Is there a problem?" asked Sachin, pursing his lips as he entered the hallway.

"No," Lazar stated evenly. He didn't want to lose his temper with Gardelle, but it was hard. "All is well. It was just a misunderstanding."

"My arse!" spat Gardelle as he shoved Lazar. "You are the chosen one to my niece, and yet you whore yourself out to every wench in the castle."

Sachin blinked and then grabbed the men each by the elbow, escorting them into one of the sitting rooms. He shut the door and pointed to Gardelle. "Explain."

Gardelle grew quiet, and Lazar knew

then the man realized his error. "Nothing. It was merely a misunderstanding."

Lazar narrowed his gaze. He knew better than to think Gardelle believed him. Gardelle simply wanted Sabrina's name kept out of it.

Sachin snorted. "Right. That is why half the castle heard you yelling?" He looked to Lazar. "What have you to say for yourself?"

"This is between Gardelle and me."

Sachin shook his head. "Not when it interferes with me training the men. Speak or I shall drag you both out to the court-yard to explain this in detail to the king who is standing before half the royal guards."

Lazar and Gardelle shared a look. That would not be good.

It was Gardelle who cleared his throat and spoke first. "I happened upon Lazar with one of the kitchen wenches."

Sachin shrugged. "He beds them nearly daily."

Gardelle clenched his fists.

Lazar stepped forward. "Not on this

day. Not for the past few days. Not since finding Sabrina again."

With an arch of his brow, Sachin put an arm out. "Do enlighten me as to why your cock has not found its way into them? It seems to favor them greatly."

He looked to Gardelle who nodded. Lazar licked his lower lip. "Because three days ago I thought my mate perished. It came to my attention she is alive and well."

Sachin's interest piqued. He put a hand on his chin. "Where is she?"

"The human realm," said Lazar quietly.

"Your mate is human as well?" Sachin asked, seeming surprised. "Have you met her? Why is she not here with you now? She is welcome here. You know that, correct?"

Lazar had to put his hands up to stop Sachin and to silence Gardelle. "Mind your voice level. Others cannot know that I know of her existence just yet."

Sachin worried his brow. "That made my head hurt, all your *others knowing of you knowing*. Why can they not know? A mate is something to be celebrated."

Gardelle lowered his head as if he knew the time had come to allow others in on his secret. "His mate is my niece."

"Niece? You have no family that I am aware of," Sachin returned.

Gardelle sighed. "I do. She's part our kind, part falconis and part human." He slid a knowing look at Sachin. "And she is currently the object of some sick game King Latravis plays. Should he learn Lazar is in her life, I fear what he would do."

Sachin took a long, measured breath before speaking. "You have a niece? She is of mixed bloodlines? And she holds favor with the enemy's king?"

"Yes," Gardelle said.

"Kabril will wish to know this. If your niece can be used to draw out the enemy king, then…"

Lazar charged Sachin, a rage like he had never experienced coming over him. He slammed the man into the wall. Anger rushed through his entire body. He wanted blood. He wanted death. "You will not use my mate to bait my brother! He is sick and twisted, and I will not stand for my woman being used to draw him out!"

Gardelle ripped Lazar from Sachin.

Sachin watched Lazar closely. He didn't act as if he were planning to attack back. "Your brother?"

Gardelle sighed. "Lazar, he must know all of it."

Lazar righted himself and nodded. This wasn't what he'd wanted. He wanted his secrets kept just that, but the time had come for truths to be exposed. He looked to Gardelle. "Kabril will have my head when the truth is revealed. Swear to me you will take Sabrina far from Latravis's reach. Swear you will keep her safe from him. Tell my little mouse that she is a thief who stole my heart with but a glance. And tell her I am sorry I was not a mate worthy of her."

Sachin raked his gaze over Lazar. "I see it now, the resemblance. Do you spy on us for your brother?"

Lazar growled. "I hate him! I would run him through with my sword and carry his head through the kingdom for all to see. He is a liar, and he rules with fear and trickery. Would I could wash his blood from my veins."

"He is not the rightful king," Gardelle stated clearly. "The rightful king of the Falcons stands before you."

Sachin nodded. "So I am coming to understand. Kabril needs to be informed of this."

"You have no reason to trust me, and you owe me no debt," Lazar said to him. "But I beg of you, assist Gardelle in getting Sabrina to safety, far from my brother's reach. Please."

"You shall do so yourself after we speak with the king." Sachin motioned for them to follow.

"Sachin, he will kill me. I am blood to his sworn enemy."

"And you saved his wife and have become a man he calls friend," Sachin reminded. "Come. Bend his ear and mayhap he can find a way to assist you."

Gardelle sighed. "He is not the only one who needs told all."

Lazar's shoulders slumped. He knew what Gardelle meant. Sabrina. She needed to know the truth. "Should the king allow me to live, I will tell her all she needs to know."

"We should tell her together," Gardelle said.

Sachin paused. "Tell me she is aware of what we are."

Lazar shook his head.

Sachin rubbed his forehead. "As her mate, you are duty bound to be truthful with her. Gardelle should not be the one now to tell her of this. Not when you are trying to forge a bond with her. The words must come from you."

"I know."

"Come, we must address the king. He needs to know of all of this," Sachin said. "And, Lazar, he will need to know if you are ready to do what must be done. If you are ready to regain your throne. The true king must rise. Are you ready?"

He'd never had the throne, so regaining it wasn't exactly right, but he didn't correct Sachin. The throne should have been his when his father passed. The same sickness that had claimed his father's mind had tainted his brother's as well. There had been no reasoning with Latravis when the seat became vacant, and Lazar never had much desire to rule a kingdom. Seeing how Latravis had cast their people into centuries of war, of dark times and death, he knew better now. He knew he had to do what must be done for his kind —for the falcons.

"I am ready," he said.

Chapter Nine

Sabrina opened the door to find Lazar there minus her uncle. She stepped back. It had been days since they'd stumbled over an excuse as to why they had to suddenly leave. Days without any word from them. She'd had it in her head to be angry, but seeing Lazar changed that. "Forget Gardelle?"

Lazar licked his lower lip. "He's still handling a few matters. He'll be here shortly. We agreed it best I return rather than leave you alone any more than we have already been forced to do."

Alarm oozed from her, but she wasn't sure why. "I'm alone all the time."

Entering the house more, Lazar eyed

her cautiously before shutting the door behind him. He locked it with a slow motion and then turned to face her. Something was wrong. Very wrong.

Sabrina's chest tightened.

"Can we talk?" asked Lazar.

"I'll make us some tea." She made an attempt to head to the kitchen, but he caught her elbow gently.

"Brina, tea will do little to ease what I need to tell you." The expression on his face scared her.

Her hand went to his forearm. "Something happened to my uncle, didn't it?"

"No," he replied. "Gardelle is well. On my flight here I had much time to think upon what you should be told and how to tell you."

"What's wrong?"

He took a deep breath and seemed to wait forever before speaking. "We should sit."

"Lazar, you're scaring me. Just say it."

He met her gaze. "You were born for me, my mate, my wife, and long ago I thought you dead. Your uncle whisked you away to live here, in this realm, among humans, away from our kind—bird shifters —for your own safety. Sabrina, know that I thought you gone, forever." He took another deep breath. "I have been unfaithful to you. I did not know you lived. That is no excuse. I know that now. My brother has wormed his way into your life, and I know not the game he plays or to what end. I do know that should Latravis be made aware that I know you live, it will not go over well."

Blinking several times, Sabrina released his arm and backed away from him slowly. She glanced to the side, trying to judge how far she was from a phone.

Man meat was bat-shit crazy. Just her luck. Sexy and shy of a full deck.

You sure know how to pick 'em.

With clear purpose Lazar stepped toward her, and fear slammed through her. He sniffed the air and froze. "You are afraid."

"No," she said a little too fast. "I'll start that tea."

He reached out quickly and caught her hand in his.

A scream escaped her.

Lazar dropped her hand as if she'd burned him. A forlorn look came over him. "My little mouse, I would never harm you. Know that."

Her lips trembled. "Okay."

"Sabrina, talk to me. Tell me why you are afraid."

"Because you're clearly crazy," she blurted.

Lazar tipped his head and grinned. "Ah, you think the tale untrue?"

"Uh, yes."

Yeah, man meat has lost it.

"Yet you have dreamed of men with wings, yes?"

Sabrina's resolve began to chip away. She had dreamed of men with wings. Specifically, Lazar with wings. She nodded.

"And you have had other dreams," he said, moving closer. "Dreams of the two of us?"

Her eyes widened.

He touched her cheek. "Of us in intimate settings?"

She yelped.

He smiled. "Sabrina, think hard. Think of all that has never made sense in your life. And think of Gardelle and how he does not understand many human customs."

"He's foreign," she protested.

Lazar merely lifted a brow. "And what of us? What of the dreams I know we have shared? The ones that have had me buried in you?"

She knew her face was at least three shades of red. Maybe more. "No. No sex dreams."

"Really?"

She gritted her teeth. "Go back to sounding crazy. I liked you better that way."

He smiled wide. "I can prove I'm telling you the truth."

"How? Going to screw me against the wall?" she snapped.

He eyed the wall and then her. "The idea is a good one."

Sabrina's legs quivered with desire. She

mentally chastised herself and then folded her arms over her chest.

Lazar touched her lower lip. "Your pout is very sexy."

"Lazar."

"Do you trust me?" he asked.

She shouldn't but she did, as crazy as he sounded. "Yes."

With a nod he turned and put his back to her. He pulled his shirt over his head, and in the blink of an eye, he was standing there with giant wings spread out as far as they could go in the foyer.

Sabrina's head felt light at the sight of them. Man meat wasn't human. "You have…wings."

LAZAR CAUGHT Sabrina and dragged her against his chest. He held her as she stirred back to consciousness. "Hello."

Her eyes widened at the sight of his wings. She pushed hard on his chest, and he freed her from his hold. She backed against the wall. "Holy crap, you have wings!"

"I do," he said. "As does your uncle and Latravis."

He thought she might scream or faint again. Instead, she eased closer to him and lifted a hand. She jerked it back right before she would have made contact with his wing. "Will it hurt? Me touching it?"

"No." He moved a wing forward, putting it closer to her.

A slight smile started upon her lips and spread wider and wider as she made contact with his feathers. His cock responded. Lazar had to clench his fists to keep from ravishing her.

Glancing at his hands, Sabrina gasped. "I hurt you." She jerked her hand back again.

Lazar caught her wrist and moved her hand back to his wing. "No. The opposite."

Her mouth dropped. "Oh. Oh!"

He grinned sheepishly. "It is very erotic to have my wings touched by my mate."

Her eyes narrowed. "Mate?"

"The woman created for me. Each shifter male is said to have one. You are basically what makes me whole. It is why we connected on the dream plane."

Sabrina watched him for the longest time and then let out a slow, shallow breath. "I'm trying very hard not to freak out right now."

"Understandable. You are being shown the truth that something more than humans exist."

She gulped. "Oddly, I'm taking the wing thing better than knowing what we've done in those dreams. Lazar, I've never done any of that with anyone before."

He drew her to him. Her arms slipped around his waist, and he held her with his arms and his wings. She snuggled against his chest. "Sabrina, you have no idea how much this pleases me."

She glanced up at him. "That I'm a virgin?"

He nodded, and his chest tightened. "I am not. You have every right to banish me from your bed. I have used endless women. I have sought to fill the hole in my heart."

She pressed her fingers to his lips.

He looked down at her just as she rose

to her tiptoes. Their lips met, and heat ignited between them. He drew his wings into himself and lifted her. He could wait no longer. She knew the truth—knew he wasn't worth her and that he could shift into a bird, and she still wanted him.

He ate at her mouth and carried her through the home. He made it to the staircase and kissed her deeper and deeper with each step. Gardelle had agreed to give him time to speak with Sabrina alone. He wasn't sure how long the warrior would deem appropriate before he came barging in, and Lazar needed to be within his mate. He could wait no more.

Sabrina stopped the kiss cold. She tensed.

"You do not want me," he said.

"I want you, but you need to know something," she replied. "While you were gone, Latravis's driver came past. Normally he only ever comes with Latravis, but this time he was alone, and something was off. He kept lingering by the door—sort of sniffing the air."

Lazar set her down at the top of the steps. "When was this?"

"Early yesterday."

Panic welled in him. Speaking with the king had taken longer than he'd wanted. While he'd intended to be gone a day at most, he'd been gone three. "Sabrina, change quickly. Put on something warm. We must go. Already he has had time to report back to Latravis that my scent was here."

She hesitated. "This is all really happening, isn't it? I'm not dreaming, am I?"

He touched her cheek tenderly. "No, *ta'konima*—my love, you're not dreaming."

A question formed on her face.

Lazar smoothed her brow. "You wonder why I called you *my love*."

"How did you know?"

He grinned. "Because I have known you since you were a child, and I have shared intimate dreams with you for the past five years. It is safe to say I know you well, Sabrina. And it is safe to say I love you."

She spun and rushed away from him. He'd have taken offense that she didn't return the words, but he'd already tossed so much at her in a short period of time. He hurried down the steps and opened the front door with the intention of scanning the skies for signs of Latravis's men.

Gardelle was there, pacing back and forth on the porch. He looked to Lazar. "I know I promised you time with her, but I thought I could help ease the news of our kind. But when I arrived, I feared what I may walk in upon. I have no wish to happen upon you bedding my niece."

"I did not bed her."

But I will. The words, while not spoken, were clear.

"I showed her the truth of what we are."

Gardelle's eyes widened. "And?"

"She fainted. She is fine now. But, Gardelle, we have a much bigger issue. Latravis knows I was here."

Gardelle gasped and shoved past him. "Sabrina! Come quickly!"

She appeared at the top of the staircase in warmer clothing as Lazar had told her to wear. "I know, and you better believe when this is all said and done you're going to explain why…" She stopped and then pointed at the open front door. "Men. Flying men!"

Lazar looked to see falcon warriors headed their way.

"Go to the basement and hide in the pantry area," Gardelle commanded. "Bolt yourself in! Go!"

"Latravis won't hurt me," she said.

Lazar sighed. "That may be true, but the men serving him would if they believed it would hurt me. Their hate of me is great. Go. Do as your uncle commands."

She nodded.

Lazar rushed out the door, to put distance between him and Sabrina before allowing his wings to release. Gardelle seized hold of him, stopping him in his tracks.

"Release me," barked Lazar. "I must lead them from her."

"And end up at the end of one of Latravis's pikes?" Gardelle demanded.

Shrugging, Lazar kept an even façade. "If it is called for."

"And what then of Brina?" Gardelle increased his hold on Lazar. "You would condemn her to a life without her mate? A life without the possibility of true love, of happiness, of maybe even a family should the bird gods look favorably upon your union as they have done for others recently?"

A family?

Lazar had never entertained the idea because it seemed an impossibility. He didn't relish the idea of leaving Sabrina alone, but he'd not risk her, and he'd do his best to avoid capture and death.

"I will go and lead them away," Gardelle said, puffing out his chest.

Lazar lurched back. "No! You are her *only* anything. Should something happen to you, she would never forgive me. She looks at you as a father figure and holds much love for you."

With that, Lazar burst into the air, his

wings emerging. Gardelle followed close at his heels. The stubborn man would not see reason even when his life depended on it.

In mere seconds the Falco warriors changed course, spotting them. There were six in all. Latravis was not one of them. That wasn't exactly optimal odds, but it could have been worse. It could have been six on one.

Lazar cast a knowing look at Gardelle.

All Falco must die. The message had to be clear. Sabrina was protected.

Gardelle nodded and charged them.

These had been men Lazar had once fought alongside. Men who now had orders to bring his head to their king. There were more of the enemy, and the enemy was armed with swords. Gardelle and Lazar simply had themselves—no weapons and no extra bodies.

Hazim, one of Latravis's henchmen, snarled and came at Lazar, his sword drawn. Lazar blocked the blow with his forearm and just missed taking a sword to the head. He struck Hazim in the chest and sent the warrior tumbling backward.

Normally, he would have followed through, going after the fallen warrior and killing him. There were too many other threats to worry about. He would have to deal with Hazim again.

Lazar twisted and extended his talons. They sliced through his fingertips, causing no pain. He swiped at another Falco warrior and caught the man by the throat. Skin seemed so fragile beneath the sharpness of Lazar's talons. The sensation was one that never ceased to surprise him, regardless of how many lives he took. The blow was a killing one. The warrior fell away, tumbling towards the ground.

Gardelle killed one as well before turning in midair and colliding with another. Hazim returned, snarling at Lazar. "You are the reason my brother is dead."

Humbert, Hazim's twin brother, had been part of the group of guards sent to find and kill the object of the King of the Hawk's affection. Lazar was one of the guards tasked with the duty. When he'd found Rayna, Kabril's mate, scared, uncertain of what was occurring and terrified of the birdmen, something within him broke. He could not obey Latravis's orders. He could not take Rayna's life. It was then he'd stepped over the line and could never return home while his brother still sat upon the throne.

"Traitor!" Hazim shouted, spittle flying from his mouth.

Hazim took another swing at Lazar, but this one was not deflected. Catching Lazar's upper shoulder, the sword cut deep. Pain radiated through his shoulder, and he turned enough to give Hazim another opening. The blade cut into Lazar's upper back. It narrowly missed taking his wing.

"Deserter!" Hate gleamed in Hazim's eyes.

Lazar thrust at him with all his might. Another warrior dove at him, sword at the ready. Lazar knew he wouldn't be fast enough to get out of the way. There was a blur, and Gardelle appeared before him. The sword pierced through Gardelle, and Lazar's breath caught.

"No!" He grabbed Gardelle. The force of the man's limp body knocked Lazar from the sky. They plummeted to the unforgiving ground. With a hard thump, Lazar struck the earth. Gardelle's limp body lay next to him.

Hazim landed with ease and stalked towards Lazar. "I will take your head to the king, and he will display it for all to see what happens to those who stand against him."

Hazim extended a hand, his talons long and ready to strike.

Lazar tried to push off the ground, but his shoulder refused to cooperate. He fell back and awaited his death, his only concern Sabrina and if the enemy would find her.

Hazim was within kill range, and Lazar exhaled slowly, prepared to meet his end. Suddenly, Hazim jerked back, his eyes wide. A long arrow stuck out from his neck. Lazar blinked and looked again. Yep. An arrow was there. Hazim held it, his hands coated in his own blood. He stared in shock at something past Lazar.

Glancing back, Lazar found Sabrina there, holding a compound bow. She already had another arrow nocked and ready to fly. She seemed like she more than knew what she was doing with the weapon. She also appeared calm. Too calm.

"Will one kill him?" she asked of Lazar, never taking her gaze from Hazim.

Lazar struggled to stand. "Brina?"

"Will he die or not?" she demanded.

"No. If one were to go through his heart as well, then yes, but—"

She sent an arrow directly into Hazim's heart. She grabbed another and prepared it. She aimed to the side, and Lazar thought it was at him.

"If you take one more step near him, I'll put this between your eyes," she said, speaking to someone else.

Lazar turned to find Ennae there, close enough to kill him. Ennae snarled at Sabrina. "Wench, we will kill him, and then we will spend endless weeks sating ourselves with your battered and broken body. He's a traitor to his people—to his king. We'll not show him or his bitch any mercy."

Lazar's attention went to Sabrina. Mavux was there, sneaking up behind her, his talons extended. He opened his mouth to shout a warning to her. She fired the arrow at Ennae, hitting his heart the first shot out. Twisting around fast, she used the bow itself as a weapon to deflect Mavux's coming blow.

With a roar, Lazar came up and off the ground. Blood dripped freely from his wounds, but he didn't care. He charged forward, throwing himself at Mavux, knocking the warrior far from Sabrina. He landed on top of him and allowed his talons to emerge once more. He went at the man's throat, removing it cleanly and efficiently. It was a wound no bird shifter could heal.

Something touched his good shoulder lightly. He tensed, and as Sabrina's scent filled his head, he relaxed, looking back at her.

Her brown eyes were moist. "You're bleeding really badly. What can I do? I'm guessing a hospital is out of the question." She stared around the scene, at what was left from the battle. Her eyes glassed over a moment as she focused on Gardelle's lifeless body. It was then he knew she was in shock.

He waited for signs she feared him. None came. He pushed to his feet and swayed. Sabrina came to him quickly, trying to assist in keeping him upright. Her body pressed to his, and he gasped, his cock unconcerned with how injured he was. It only cared about having her close.

She stared up at him, her tiny hands going to his neck and jaw. "Gardelle is…" She teared up. "He's not moving. I can't do it. I can't look. I can't know…"

He knew Gardelle was seriously wounded but still alive. His sensitive hearing picked up the faintest sounds of a heartbeat. What he wasn't sure of was if Yosim was still near or if he'd fled to alert the others of Lazar's location. "Sabrina, the other—the last of the winged men. Did you see where he went?"

She nodded, the tears breaking free

from her. "He went up, high in the sky, that way." She pointed towards the portal.

Lazar closed his eyes a second. "I have to get you to safety. He'll return with others—too many for me to protect you against."

"We can't leave Gardelle," she said, crying harder. "Please, Lazar."

As she pushed tighter against him, his resolve crumbled. He found himself giving in to her when he knew better. It wasn't safe to remain. Still, he couldn't deny her.

"Go inside. I will retrieve Gardelle. We'll need to cleanse his wounds. If any soil or dirt from your realm managed to find its way into them, he'll not be able to heal."

"He's not dead?"

"No, but the risk to him is great. Can you do as I ask?"

She nodded. "I'll gather supplies. Can you lift him? You're hurt and—"

He dipped his head, his lips finding hers. The kiss was chaste but still moved him. He panted and pulled back. "I will be fine. Go."

Chapter Ten

Sabrina sat at Gardelle's bedside. He'd not so much as moved since Lazar had carried him in and assisted in cleaning his wounds. Her throat was tight as she held her uncle's hand. So much had been thrown at her at once that she wasn't sure if she'd gone mad or not. One second her uncle's handsome friend was stopping by, and the next, everyone but her seemed to have wings and a death wish.

A loud thump from the adjoining bathroom caught her attention. She went quickly to it and rapped lightly on the door. "Lazar?"

He didn't answer, and something deep inside her told her he wasn't as fine as he'd pretended to be. Turning the handle, she opened the door.

"Lazar," she repeated, wanting to afford him privacy but wishing to help if need be as well. She pushed the door open more and peeked her head in.

Lazar's muscular form was on the floor, half in and half out of the garden tub. She hardly noticed he was naked. All she noticed was the large gaping wound on his upper back, near his shoulder. Muscle and bone were exposed. In addition, dirt and mud was smeared in it as well. She wasted no time as she ran to his side and bent, assuring his face wasn't under the line of water in the tub.

He came to, slightly dazed. "Hmm?"

She smoothed his hair back from his face. "Your back... You're hurt. Bad. It's full of dirt."

His eyelids fluttered closed, and she tapped his cheeks lightly.

"Lazar."

He looked at her.

"Either you find a way to help me get you into that tub, or so help me God I'll call Lisa for help. I'm not going to let you die to protect your secret."

She tugged on him, and he rose enough to slide into the tub. The thing had been designed for Gardelle, so it was enormous. Lazar instantly sank under, and Sabrina reacted, climbing in after him, standing over him and positioning him so he was reclined against the back, his head out of the water.

It took a second for her to realize she was straddling a naked man's waist, her dress hiked high. The only thing between the two of them was her now-soaked panties.

Strong hands clamped down on her hips, locking her in place. Gasping, she looked to find Lazar's eyes open and his gaze hungry. Color stained her face as his cock lengthened, hardening beneath her.

His breathing was labored, and she wasn't sure if it was from what was happening between them or if it was from how injured he was.

Maybe even both.

"You're hurt," she managed. For some

strange reason, she leaned, putting her face even closer to his.

His lips took hold of hers, and she squirmed on his lap. His tongue darted into her mouth, and she moaned, her entire body tightening in response. As much as her body and even her mind wanted to give herself to this man—she knew it wasn't right. He was hurt. He needed to heal.

Sabrina tore her mouth free of his and panted. "We need to get your wounds clean too."

He tried to kiss her again, but she put her hand over his mouth, stopping him. Amusement lit his dark eyes.

"First I help fix you and then you can fuck me." She snapped her lips shut, her eyes wide. "I mean…umm."

Lazar smiled against her palm. He pulled her hand from his mouth. "Too late. A promise is a promise."

A tiny laugh bubbled up from her. "You're in no condition to be doing anything, so cut that randy look off your face, buddy. Let's get you cleaned up and then you need to rest too."

"I will be fine, Sabrina," he said, looking hungrily at her lips.

She traced the edges of his jaw with her fingers. "I take it you've been stubborn since birth too, huh? Is it a guy-with-wings thing?"

He watched her closely. "You were to remain in the basement. You do not listen well, little mouse."

She exhaled slowly. "I went there. Then I freaked out about the two of you alone against all those men."

He ran his hand to the back of her hair and pulled the tie from it. "So you decided to arm yourself and save us?"

"Yes and no," she admitted. "I just thought I'd slow them down a little, but mostly I wasn't thinking too clearly. I was worried something would happen to you."

Lazar caressed her neck. "I will live."

"Good," she whispered, and kissed his lips tenderly.

He grinned. "The bow?"

She bit at her lower lip. "Is Gardelle's."

"He taught you to shoot it?" Lazar asked, surprise evident in his voice.

"Oh no," she said. "He's always had a strict   no-touching-of-his-weapons-collection rule. Someone else taught me."

Lazar   stiffened   beneath   her. "Latravis?"

She considered lying to him, but decided against it. He'd been through enough already. "Yes."

Silence thickened the air between them.

"Never thought I'd use any of the skills I learned. Never thought my uncle had wings either." She took a moment. "Wait a minute? Do I have wings too?"

Lazar's smile widened. "No. But, before you ask, Gardelle is your biological uncle. You are the daughter of his half-sister. She did not possess the ability to shift forms either."

"And my father?" she questioned. "Was he like you and Gardelle?"

"Yes, though more like me than Gardelle. He was a *Falco Peregrinus*, not a *Buteo Regalis*."

"Oh." She inclined her head. "Okay, I don't know what that means."

His thumb eased over her lower lip. "One is a falcon and the other a royal hawk."

As she concentrated on what he was saying, her jaw dropped. "You shift into a falcon?"

"Yes."

"And Gardelle can shift into a hawk?"

He nodded.

She kissed the pad of his thumb without thought and put her hands up to about the size of a falcon. "But how do you get so small?"

Lazar's deep laugh seemed to wrap around her. "Sabrina, we do not end up the size of the falcons and hawks who inhabit the human realm. We are much, much bigger. Some of us are able to minimize our shifted form for short lengths, but it requires a great deal of power and concentration to hold a form anything close to as small as the birds here."

"Does it hurt?" she asked. "When you turn into a bird?"

"No. Denying a shift or going for long periods without permitting one's wings to emerge causes discomfort."

Sabrina made a move to stand, but Lazar held her to him. "I need to clean your back and shoulder. And I don't think I should press my luck by sitting on your lap much longer."

"Afraid I will ravish you?"

"Kind of hopeful you will, and that is freaking me out more than the birdman thing."

He kissed the tips of his fingers and pressed them to her lips gently. "Then I will control myself until you are ready to accept all of me."

She tensed.

"Sabrina."

"Y-yes?"

"You *will* accept all of me very soon," he said evenly.

She licked her lips. "I know."

"Good girl," he said drawing her closer to him. His lips found hers once more, and his kiss was just as explosive as before. She tried to pull free, but he refused to allow her. She was actually glad.

Opening her mouth, she surrendered, giving him greater access to her. His tongue caressed hers, easing around it just right to make her inner thighs tighten. She wanted even more than he was offering. She took hold of the sides of his face and deepened the level of their kiss. Lazar's arms shot out. Grabbing the tub, Lazar tensed, his entire body flexed under her. She kept going, kept making love to his mouth with hers.

He pushed up, his hips grinding against hers. His erection struck her mound, hitting it in a spot that left her moaning into his mouth. She sucked on his tongue, and he thrust upward, holding himself there, his cock jerking.

Sabrina stilled, her lips against his. She knew he'd ejaculated, and the knowledge her kiss had brought him to it gave her a profound sense of satisfaction. She pulled herself from his mouth and kissed the tip of his nose. "I'm thinking I need to change into dry clothes and you need fresh bathwater before we clean that wound on your back."

Lazar stared up at her, heaving. He swallowed hard and nodded.

Fear that he regretted what had happened washed over her. She averted her eyes and stood quickly. Lazar rose too, and she thought he'd fall. Water streamed off his body, and she couldn't help but look down. His cock was huge. Her eyes widened at the sight of it.

Lazar touched her chin, lifting her gaze to his face. He dipped his head and pressed a tender kiss to her lips. "Hurry back, Sabrina."

She grinned. "Promise not to pass out while I'm gone. I don't want to come back and find you've drowned."

He winked. "I promise."

———

LAZAR WOKE to find Sabrina tucked safely against his body. He remembered her returning to the bathroom and assisting in cleaning his back and then her leading him to a guest bedroom, but nothing beyond that. As much as he'd wanted to deny it, his wound had been grave and had taken all of his strength to begin to heal.

Sabrina's breathing was light, barely there, as she slept. Her lithe frame fit snugly against him. His arm was over her hip and his hand splayed across her abdomen. He had never actually spent an entire night with one woman in his hundreds of years, and he most certainly had never awoken with one—cuddling.

As repulsed as he'd have thought he'd have been by the idea, he found he enjoyed it greatly. Though he suspected it had something to do with which female was in the bed with him.

Sabrina.

In her own right, she was a warrior. She'd saved both his and Gardelle's lives by taking a stance and taking out a Falco warrior. She'd also refused to back down and run. She'd remained, tending to them both, never showing weakness. He knew she was worried about both him and Gardelle. He could sense it on her.

He brushed the hair from her shoulder and planted a tiny kiss to her exposed, creamy flesh. His cock showed signs of life, and he willed it down. He'd not take her just yet. He'd give her the time she required before he claimed what was rightfully his.

In addition, he needed to assure she was safe before he dared to mark her as his own. Already the enemy would seek to harm her in order to get at him—if she was his wife, his mate, the torture she would endure would be indescribable.

Lazar eased himself from the bed, careful not to wake her. His pants were clean and laying across the back of a chair at the foot of the bed. He wondered how long she'd stayed up handling everything after he'd succumbed to the healing sleep.

He reached for the pants, and something skimmed his back lightly. He twisted to find Sabrina there, looking at him. "You're going to leave without saying goodbye, aren't you?"

He stared at her for the longest time. "I was going to leave to avoid ravishing you. You deserve better than me. More than I can give you."

She ran her hand down his back and then up again. "It's healed."

He nodded. "Thanks to you."

"Lazar?" she asked, her voice soft and sweet.

He wanted to kiss her. "Yes?"

"Stay."

"Sabrina."

She shocked him by pulling her night-gown off and tossing it aside. She was left sitting there in nothing more than thin panties. Her breasts called to him, making need slam through his aching body. There was no denying her.

His body burned for her. He closed the distance between them. With manly pride he tugged her to him and dipped his head, taking possession of her mouth. She didn't fight him. She wrapped her arms around his neck.

His body was sore, but he didn't care. He had his mate in his arms. Their tongues met, and he lifted her, walking her to the bed. The time had come. He would wait no more.

EXCITEMENT MOVED through Sabrina as Lazar laid her out on the bed. He stepped back and removed his pants. She'd seen him naked both in the tub and in her dreams and already had a very good idea of what he'd feel like in her. She didn't want to confess to him that she'd never allowed another to this point. Somehow, deep down, she knew Lazar would find a way to deny her pleasure once more, and Sabrina was having none of that. Come hell or high water, man meat was going to be with her if she had to clunk him over the head and take advantage of him to do it.

She relaxed as he skimmed his hands over her stomach to the top of her panties. Tugging them down her legs, he offered a seductive look before tossing her panties aside and focusing on her sex. He pushed her legs open wide. Cool air skated over her sex, and her first instinct was to close her legs. Lazar was having none of that. He shook his finger at her with a sexy-assin grin upon his handsome face. Dipping his head, he exhaled, his lips found her clit, and she cried out the minute his tongue slid over the swollen bud. Pleasure trickled throughout her lower region. She felt wanton and wild. Exactly like he'd made her feel in her dreams.

She moaned as his gifted tongue worked its magik on her cunt. She'd never felt so free, so liberated. She loved it. Loved the sensations he was providing her. Tipping her head, Sabrina dug her fingers into the sheets, tugging at them as her body tightened around Lazar. The pleasure danced up her inner thighs at first before slinking its way to her midriff. It focused there. Heat building. Pressure mounting. She thought she'd burst. Pulling harder at the sheets, she moaned and writhed beneath him, wiggling to the point he practically pinned her with his arms.

He dipped a finger into her and her body immediately tried to push out the intrusion. Lazar seemed pleased. He dipped his finger in more, breaking through her virginal barrier. The pain was fast and fleeting. She rocked on his hand as his mouth continued to work her clit. Sabrina stared down at him. His blond hair was like a veil, covering his eyes. She pushed it away, her fingers skimming his forehead. How could a man be so sexy, so alluring and so tortured on the inside all at one time? She wanted to soothe away his worry. She wanted to right all the wrongs in his life. Mostly, she wanted to love him and be loved by him.

Lazar lifted his head from her pussy and kissed her fingertips. His chin glistened with her cream. The emotions she felt for him crashed through her at the same moment his finger found her sweet spot. Her jaw dropped as a strangled cry of pleasure released from her. Her pussy clenched involuntarily around his finger, and her legs drew in, tightening on his shoulders.

Lazar eased his finger from her body, and she nearly moaned at the loss of it. As he slid up and over her, she opened her legs more to him. He stroked his engorged cock and dipped his head, sucking on her nipple. He jerked on his shaft.

Sabrina touched the sides of his face. "Please, Lazar. I need you in me."

"Sabrina of the Hawks and of the Falcons, do you accept me—all of me—from now until the end of time?"

She stilled. "What?"

He refused to give her what she wanted—him. "You must answer, *ta'konima.*"

"W-what?"

"Answer," he said, mischief in his eyes.

"Yes. Oh God, yes."

"Very good."

He moved from one nipple to the other, and she thought for sure her body would somehow burn up. That she would ignite and there would be nothing but ash left to show for what he'd done to her. The pleasures he'd given.

He lined his cock head up with her core and took a deep breath. Lazar's lips found hers. His kiss chased away her nerves. She opened her legs more for him, and he entered in one quick, long thrust. She moaned, and he ate away the sounds, his body affecting hers. They were one.

She clawed at his arms as he pushed into her, slow at first. He kept time, pumping in and out, in and out. She panted into his mouth and moved her hips, wanting what he was giving to be harder and faster. His lips twitched against hers as he smiled slightly. He gave in to her unspoken plea. He thrust hard into her again and again until she no longer knew what was happening. She only knew that every ounce of her was tingling, waiting on the edge of exploding.

He drilled her into the bed and into sweet oblivion. She thrashed at the sheets, not wanting to claw at Lazar's arms any more than she already had. Soon the pleasure was too much. She broke the kiss and cried out as her orgasm washed over her, making her legs shake and her pussy clench around his cock.

Lazar roared before pushing and holding deep within her. She felt his cock twitching as his seed emptied into her. She wrapped her legs tighter around him, wanting him to never leave her body.

He kissed the tip of her nose.

She smiled up at him and then caressed his cheek.

He closed his eyes and tipped his head into her palm. He sighed and then kissed her palm tenderly.

LAZAR STAYED THERE ABOVE HER, kissing her lazily. He never wanted to leave the haven of her body. Not now that she was his. He'd come in her. She'd agreed to his verbal claim as well. He'd forged the bond with her. She'd been different from the other women. So much more. He could never want another, not after having her.

Sabrina smiled against his lips. "That was totally worth waiting so long for."

He snickered. "I'm pleased that you are pleased. And I agree, it was very, very, very good. We should do it again and soon."

She laughed softly, her hands skimming

his back. "Okay, but only if you have your wings out next time. I want to touch them."

"Brina," he said. "You understand what happened between us, don't you?"

"We had sex, man meat."

"Man meat?"

Her lips twitched. "Never mind. Yes. I know what happened. We had sex."

He nodded. "More than that, though. Do you understand what it means?"

She bit her lower lip. "I'm guessing a lot more than I think it does."

"Yes," he said. "For our kind, what we did, what we shared, it's a bonding ritual—what occurs between a mated pair."

He saw the confusion in her eyes.

"Brina, you are mine now. In the eyes of our people, you are my wife. I know I'm not what you'd want. I have no title, nothing to give you. I will understand if you refuse to return to my realm with me and if you do not wish for me to remain here with you."

She looked at him for the longest time and then surprised him by kissing him gently. "Lazar, I don't care about titles. And I don't know about returning to your realm. It's all so sudden. But I don't want to be separated from you. I know that much."

"Good, because we will not be separated. Not now. Not ever." He exhaled slowly. "Sabrina, Latravis will retaliate for the men he lost."

She bit her lower lip and nodded. "I know. But, Lazar, maybe, just maybe, we could sit down and talk with him. He's not all bad, is he?"

Lazar didn't want to argue with her. He didn't want to go into detail that the Hawks were now ready to launch a full-scale attack against the Falcons to remove Latravis from the throne and seat Lazar upon it. For now he just wanted to love his mate and allow her to live in ignorant bliss. The harsh realities of the war to come didn't need to spoil their moment. They'd be living it soon enough.

A knock sounded from the door below. Lazar sniffed the air.

Sachin and the others had arrived.

Sabrina would need to return to his realm, like it or not. He just hoped his young wife was willing. Abducting her would be no way to start off their lives together.

"Who is here?" she asked.

He kissed the tip of her nose. "Friends. The time has come to return to my homeland. You and Gardelle will come."

She didn't argue. That was a good sign.

Chapter Eleven

SABRINA STARED AROUND IN ABSOLUTE wonder at the castle. Already it felt as if she'd fallen through the rabbit hole while being flown by Lazar to this place. This land that wasn't anything like the one she'd spent her life growing up in. He'd called it a name. Something that started with an A, but all she got out of it was *so not friggin' Earth*.

She shivered. Lazar drew her back against his frame and rubbed her arms. "You are cold?" he asked.

She shook her head. He'd assured she'd dressed warmly for the flight and had talked her through much of it before they actually took off. Her gaze wandered to the other birdmen. The ones who had arrived at her home, handled the dead bodies of the other bad men and carried Gardelle all the way to the castle they stood in now.

The one with the deepest accent kept eyeing her. He had a twin who hadn't said a word yet. "She is very tiny."

"She is, my lord," said Lazar.

My lord?

Right. King. Yes. Lazar had called him the king before. She leaned back more into Lazar's arms. "Do I have to bow or something?"

The king chuckled. "If you dared try, I fear my wife would take vital pieces from me."

"Damn straight," a woman with long dark hair said as she entered the throne room. She held herself with an air that said she was in a position of power but she wasn't untouchable. In fact, she kept coming straight at Sabrina. The woman put her arms out and yanked Sabrina into a hug.

"It's so good to have another woman

here. We're so far from evening the numbers," she said. "You could choke on the testosterone around this joint."

Sabrina just stood there, letting the woman hug her.

"This is Rayna, the queen," Lazar said softly.

"Queen, *smeen*," the woman mocked. "I'm just Rayna. I see you've met Kabril, Aeson, Sachin and Rosi—or Iorgos when he gets his way. Word to the wise, don't give him his way."

One of the men groaned. She guessed that might be Rosi.

Sabrina stared at the other men. She couldn't point out who was who if someone paid her.

Rayna laughed and hooked her arm through Sabrina's. "I'll make them all wear nametags if it will help."

"Oh, could you?" she blurted.

The queen laughed more.

Sabrina blushed. "You're not what I expected a bird queen to be."

Rayna lifted her brows. "Sweetie, I'm human. I couldn't shift if my life depended on it, and I wouldn't want to. I leave the heavy lifting to the boys here. I suggest you do the same. They like it. Makes 'em feel manly and all."

Sabrina liked the woman instantly. She reminded her of Lisa.

A pang of guilt came over her. She'd never see Lisa again.

Rayna leaned and put her lips to Sabrina's ear. "Give them time to get a handle on what is happening with the Falcons and then we can take some trips home, okay?"

She gasped. "You read minds?"

"Pfft, no. You're not the first woman they've yanked from the flip side. You won't be the last. Come on, I'll introduce you to Paige and Shelby. They will love you."

She looked back at Lazar, and he nodded to her. "Go with Rayna, *ta'konima*. She can take you to see where Gardelle is being treated by the healers."

She followed the queen.

LAZAR WAITED until the women were gone and focused on the king and the others. "The attack was brutal. Gardelle was wounded gravely."

Sachin nodded. "He will heal. It will take time."

"There is a human woman I believe he will want guarded while he heals," Lazar added. "Her name is Lisa. She is close friends with my mate and I believe important to Gardelle in ways he is not yet willing to admit."

Kabril snapped his fingers and other guards appeared. "Arrange for flight to the human realm. You will watch over a human there from afar. I will get the details to you soon."

They nodded and headed off.

"Thank you," said Lazar.

"It is the least one king could do for a fellow king," he said, his gaze even. "Lazar, a great battle will come upon us soon."

"I know. It is my fight, my lord. I will go and rally those still loyal to me and…"

Kabril lifted a hand, silencing him. "You are one of us now, whether or not you see it. We stand together. We remove Latravis from the throne as one, and we help to seat you upon it together. Understood?"

Sachin snorted. "Way to give him a lot of choice."

Kabril shrugged. "We're all stubborn. Doesn't matter what bird form we shift into."

Lazar smiled, feeling at home for the first time in a long time. The fight would be long and hard, but the time had come. It had to be done. With Kabril's help, Lazar could assure Sabrina was safe while he did what must be done—kill his brother.

THE END

Note to readers: Author recommends reading Prince of Pleasure next for max reading enjoyment. Buy Link for Prince of Pleasure

Complimentary Material

The following material is free of charge. It will never affect the price of your book.

Prince of Pleasure
Blurb

Prince of Pleasure

Book Five in the King of Prey series.

Youngest born in a family of royal hawk shifters, Rossi is used to dodging responsibility and doing what he wishes. His needs are simple—he likes fighting, and bedding beautiful women. He isn't looking for a mate, so when his meddlesome sister-in-law decides to divine his future, he's stunned to find out he's about to meet her —the one. His mate. And she's human.

As one who does his best to limit his time in the human realm, Rossi believes there is no chance he'll cross paths with the woman destiny has in store for him. After all, it's not as if humans fall from the sky in the realm of bird shifters.

Or do they?

Click to buy Prince of Pleasure **today!**

Excerpt: Prince of Pleasure

CHAPTER ONE

Human Realm

"Here birdie, birdie, birdie," Lucy Navarre whispered in a not-so hushed tone as she moved through the woods just outside the small town she'd been calling home by way of an efficiency apartment for the past three weeks. Her actual home wasn't really much of one, but she liked it well enough. Not that one could grow too accustomed to an off-campus condo being home when one was forced to share it with three other girls.

Somehow, she had.

She was on borrowed time and funds. Soon, the money she'd made by slinging hash at the diner just a few blocks from the university she attended would be spent. She needed to get her proof and then get back home. Back to her crappy job dealing with drunken, rowdy fraternity brothers as they left bars at closing time and stumbled into the diner wanting food.

Lucy did what she had to do to make ends meet as a full-time student with an expensive hobby—investigating and documenting the paranormal. She was determined to prove more than the normal, everyday, garden-variety paranormal investigator. Lately, there seemed to be as many experts on the paranormal as there were lawyers. She knew far too many paranormal sleuths who were self-proclaimed experts in the field. And nearly all of them claimed they were scientific in their approach.

Yeah, sure they were.

She had no interest in trying to contact the dead.

Been done.

And there were about fifty shows on television at any given moment doing it as well.

Boring.

And, really, where was the excitement in doing the same thing everyone else was doing? She wanted something more. Something that everyone and their brother weren't doing.

She wanted proof of the existence of bird shifters—men who could sprout huge wings and take flight, but who looked like humans any other time. Her guardians had told stories about them when she was a child. Lucy had hung on their every word, committing each tale to memory. She could still recite the tales to this day. Still hear the slow, southern drawl of the man she'd called Pappy telling her all about the men who were like angels, yet sinned like demons when permitted—as any man would, Pappy would say with a wink.

Pappy had even taken her on hunting expeditions when she was little, the end goal being to see and log data on birdmen. They'd been successful too. She didn't care if everyone thought they were nuts—she'd been there with him. She'd seen what he'd seen.

Men with wings.

"Majestic beings," she said softly, still remembering every detail of the men—one in particular. They'd left an impression on her.

When the elderly couple, who had cared for her after the death of her mother when Lucy was only five, passed away, Lucy found herself alone. She'd desperately wanted one of the winged men to appear and whisk her away to somewhere safe and warm. Somewhere she could see her loved ones again. That never happened. Instead, at eleven she'd ended up as part of the state of Mississippi's foster care system.

She didn't want to think any more on it.

For now, she'd concentrate on what had gotten her through it all—thinking of ways to prove the existence of the bird-men. The nagging need to fill a void she'd had for nearly a decade had become all-consuming, and she'd decided to fill it with researching the tales of the birdmen. Of proving they were real.

"Tonight is the night," she said, her voice cutting through the silence that seemed shrouded in darkness around her.

There should have been something making noise.

Anything.

There was nothing.

Except her.

And that was far from normal. There should have been the sounds of insects, of the breeze blowing through the leaves, of wildlife, anything. Not utter silence.

She grinned. "That's it birdies, show yourselves."

All the signs pointed to this night being the one where she finally got the proof she so desperately sought. Well, the signs were really hunches she felt in her gut, but she was willing to bank on them. They'd served her well in the past.

Her cell buzzed and she took it from her pocket, glancing at the screen. Alice, one of her three roommates, was texting again, wanting to know if she was done playing in the woods hunting fake men with wings, and if she wanted a ticket to a local rock band playing back home tomorrow. If it hadn't been markedly cheaper to split the cost of a condo four ways than it was to pay room and board at the university, she'd have forgone the entire thing— opting for solitude and no meddling friends. As it was, her pockets were not deep enough to warrant a private room. She took what she could get.

Lucy sighed.

Alice and the others simply did not understand her or her ways. Though Alice did try. Lucy had to give her credit for that. Mary Ellen and Amber Lynn made no effort to even try.

No surprise.

They were more worried about planning their next mani-pedi party than they were about anything else in life. Their grade point average reflected as much. Damn shame their professors didn't quiz them on the season's hottest nail polish colors. They'd have gotten top marks, for sure.

Alice and Lucy had other goals. Alice was studying business with the hope of launching her own company, and Lucy was finishing up a pre-law undergraduate degree, wanting to go on to law school when she was done. In the meantime, she was putting in all the time she could on her hobby.

So close to finding answers, she texted Alice.

Stay safe, Alice returned.

Always.

Try not to capture anything we can't house-train, replied Alice.

Lucy laughed as she texted, *So that is a no to the Lockness monster?*

Will it fit in the tub?

Before Lucy could reply, Alice sent, *Ever thought of spending your Friday night looking for a boyfriend? When is the last time you had sex?*

Lucy cringed. *I don't remember.*

My point exactly.

Lucy laughed again and put her phone in her jacket pocket. She really did need to find a man and soon. Though, that wasn't exactly easy. The guys who went to her school preferred skinny girls to her.

Her flashlight cut through the darkness. Most sane women did not venture into the woods, at night, alone, in search of things that could, in theory, be dangerous. Though she didn't believe they would be. If Lucy was correct, and she was betting her life she was, what she sought was peaceful and misunderstood. In her short time in the small town, she'd already managed to develop something of a reputation as being anything but sane or rational.

The crazy girl who hunted for monsters that weren't real.

At least according to their narrow minds.

She didn't care.

She knew better.

She was a woman on a mission, and she could sense deep down that she was close to making a breakthrough. It was the perfect time to delve deeper. The semester had ended at college and the next wasn't due to start for nearly six weeks. Plenty of time to try to prove her theory.

Her professors even questioned her interest in her "hobby"—as they called it —cryptology. But she enjoyed it immensely. It filled a void for her, one she'd had from an early age. It wouldn't pay the bills; the law someday would—at least, she hoped. She was in her junior year, but had at least another year and half to go. She'd be a fifth year senior, for sure.

She sighed. So many students were anymore.

She tried to take as many classes as she could to make her money stretch—since the cost was the same for her to take twelve or nineteen credit hours. Apparently full-time was full-time. And she would prob-ably be closer to completion if she took interim courses and classes over the summer, but her passion demanded she give it her attention as well.

She didn't fall into the habits of some who took up the torch of studying what most believed didn't exist. No. Bigfoot and the Moth Man weren't her thing. She took an altogether different path. One far less traveled.

Men who could shift into birds.

The "birdies" she was hunting.

History was littered with sightings and reports from eyewitnesses. Some labeled what they saw as angels or even demons. She believed the men were something else entirely. From what she'd pieced together, they were real and they weren't gods or anything of the sort, but rather beings that had come and gone freely since the dawn of time.

She'd found patterns in the sightings. Narrowed down the best possible locations to perhaps catch a look at them herself and document proof of their existence. With her camera at the ready, she pushed deeper into the woods.

The bite of fall was in the air and Lucy was pleased she'd had the forethought to bundle up prior to heading out. Still, her cheeks and nose were cold. She ignored the discomfort and continued on. She'd get her proof and others would stop laughing at her.

She was no one's joke.

The temperature dropped even more with each step she took deeper into the woods. She pulled her jacket tighter, thankful she'd paired it with one of her university sweatshirts. The *Rebs* logo was faded and worn—the mark of a well-loved article of clothing. She'd spent three comfy years donning it whenever she could— wearing it while studying for exams or when she noticed all her roommates were out on dates while she was back at the shared condo reading the latest and greatest on the newest chupacabra sight- ings. The sweatshirt was something of a security blanket for her. It was there for her when men weren't. And it didn't give a rat's ass what size she was.

Unlike men.

Alice was right. She did need to find a guy. One who didn't care that she wasn't a stick figure. That she actually enjoyed eating and, unlike some of the girls she knew, didn't rush to the bathroom to expel anything she ate.

"Fat chance I'm finding a prince

charming who likes curves," she mused, walking onward. Her sex-starved body would have to wait. She was a girl on a mission and she wasn't stopping it for anything—not even the quest to get laid. Besides, the men she met never lived up to her idea of Prince Charming. They lacked something he had.

Wings.

She smiled as she thought about the birdman that had captured her attention when she was young. He'd been unbelievably handsome. Not to mention, he could fly.

What little girl wouldn't grow up with a secret crush on him? Now a young woman, she found it hard to be bothered with human men. Not when she knew the truth of what was out there.

Soon, everyone would know about them.

A tiny pang of worry filled her gut. What if she'd imagined the birdmen? What if Pappy's stories had been so vivid, so compelling to her that she'd allowed herself to think she'd seen a majestic creature with wings?

"No," she said. "They're real. I know it. *He's* real."

When she came to a clearing, she paused, staying to the tree line as she clicked off her flashlight and took a seat. This was it. The spot she could trace several sightings back to. She'd been here before, more than once. Nothing had come of it, but that didn't matter. She knew in her gut this was where she needed to be.

Something rustled the leaves on the other side of the clearing. She brought her camera up and waited. Excitement churned in her stomach, heightening her senses. She watched, positive this was the moment she'd spent years waiting for. The smell of pine needlcs increased to the point that it was sickening.

Another rustle of leaves sounded.

She put her finger over the button to snap a picture, fully prepared to have her moment. When a raccoon wandered out from the other side of the clearing, her heart sank. She let out a breath she'd been unaware she was holding and then pulled her finger away from the button on her camera.

Darn.

She'd been so sure.

"What do we have here?" a deep voice asked from behind her, startling her, making her drop her camera as she spun around. The camera went off, as did its flash, illuminating two rather large males, each shirtless, wearing leather bottoms and boots that were unlike any boots she'd ever seen. She bent, grabbing her camera and clutching it to her.

Lucy took a step backwards and lost her footing, her legs going out from under her as one of the muscle-bound men reached for her with an unearthly quickness. There was a loud fluttering sound accompanied by a blur of black that seemed to wall up behind the men.

No. Not a wall, she thought, her mind racing.

Wings.

She gasped, stunned she'd been successful to such a degree. Not only that, seeing them again in the flesh meant she'd not been crazy, she'd not hallucinated or allowed an overactive imagination to guide her.

They were real.

She had thought she'd obtain grainy photos of something birdman-like moving far off in the distance. But here they were; birdmen, up close and personal.

Birdmen with huge black wings that were wider than the men were tall. It took her a second to catch up with what was happening and who the men were. She'd been expecting something more bird-like and less guys-who-live-at-the-gym types, but she'd take anything. "You're them!"

"Sure, wench," one said snidely, his accent thicker than the other. "I will be whatever you want me to be."

"Grab her!" the other shouted.

The man seized hold of her arm roughly and discomfort found her quickly.

"Ouch! I only want a picture," she said, the ground suddenly moving out from under her. Lucy's camera dropped free of her grasp and crashed to the unforgiving ground with a sickening thud that echoed deep in her chest. That camera had cost her nearly six months' worth of tips, and she'd been so excited when she'd bought it two years back. Now it was in pieces, appearing to get farther and farther from her.

No. It's not moving, she thought. *I am.*

For a split second, she didn't understand what was happening. When the realization hit her, she was pretty sure she screamed, yet she couldn't hear a sound as she was whisked high into the skies by the very birdmen she'd wanted picture proof of.

Her thoughts didn't instantly go to panic or even elation that her adoptive caregivers had been right, as had she. Her focus settled on one undeniable fact.

"Holy crap! You're real and you're douchebags!"

CLICK TO BUY Prince of Pleasure **today!**

About the Author

Dear Reader

Did you enjoy this title and want to know more about Mandy M. Roth, her pen names and all the titles she has available for purchase (over 100)?

About Mandy:

New York Times & *USA TODAY* Bestselling Author Mandy M. Roth is a self-proclaimed Goonie, loves 80s music and movies and wishes leg warmers would come back into fashion. She also thinks the movie The Breakfast Club should be mandatory viewing for...okay, everyone. When she's not dancing around her office to the sounds of the 80s or writing books, she can be found designing book covers for New York publishers, small presses, and indie authors.

Learn More:

To learn more about Mandy and her pen names, please visit www.MandyRoth.com

For latest news about Mandy's newest releases and sales subscribe to her newsletter: Sign Up For Mandy's Newsletter

Want to see all Mandy's books? Click here.

Printable PDF list of all Mandy's titles: Click here.

To join Mandy's Facebook Reader Group: The Roth Heads.

Review this title:

Please let others know if you enjoyed this title. Consider leaving an honest review on the vendor site in which you purchased this title. Reviews help to spread the word and boost overall sales. This means more books in the series you love.

Thank you!

facebook.com/AuthorMandyRoth

twitter.com/mandymroth

instagram.com/mandymroth

goodreads.com/mandymroth

pinterest.com/mandymroth

bookbub.com/authors/mandy-m-roth

youtube.com/mandyroth

amazon.com/author/mandyroth

Featured Titles from Mandy M. Roth

The Immortal Ops Series World
Immortal Ops
Critical Intelligence
Radar Deception
Strategic Vulnerability
Tactical Magik
Act of Mercy
Administrative Control
Act of Surrender
Broken Communication
Separation Zone
Act of Submission
Damage Report
Act of Command
Wolf's Surrender
The Dragon Shifter's Duty

Midnight Echoes
Isolated Maneuver
Expecting Darkness
Area of Influence
Act of Passion
Act of Brotherhood
Healing the Wolf
Wrecked Intel
And more to come…

Cozy Paranormal Mysteries
Once Hunted, Twice Shy
Total Eclipse of the Hunt
Don't Stop Bewitching
And more to come…

Tempting Fate Series
Loup Garou
Bad Moon Rising
And more to come…

The Guardians Series
The Guardians
Crossing Hudson
Ruling Jude
And more to come…

The Druid Series
Sacred Places
Goddess of the Grove
Winter Solstice
A Druid of Her Own
And more to come…

The King of Prey Series
King of Prey
A View to a Kill
Master of the Hunt
Rise of the King
Prince of Pleasure
Prince of Flight

Bureau of Paranormal Investigation (BPI)
Hunted Holiday
Heated Holiday

Prospect Springs Shifters
Blaze of Glory
Parker's Honor
Gabe's Fortune

CPSIA information can be obtained
at www.ICGtesting.com
Printed in the USA
LVOW10s1551230518
578229LV00001B/219/P